AMERICAN ADVENTURES

Luke

AMERICAN ADVENTURES

Luke

1849—On the Golden Trail

BONNIE PRYOR

ILLUSTRATED BY
BERT DODSON

Morrow Junior Books

NEW YORK

Published by Morrow Junior Books
a division of William Morrow and Company, Inc.
1350 Avenue of the Americas, New York, NY 10019
www.williammorrow.com

Printed in the United States of America.

10   9   8   7   6   5   4   3   2   1

Library of Congress Cataloging-in-Publication Data
Pryor, Bonnie.
Luke: 1849—on the golden trail / Bonnie Pryor; illustrated by Bert Dodson.
p. cm.—(American adventures)
Summary: In 1849 eleven-year-old Luke leaves his family's farm home in Iowa,
accepts his uncle's offer of a chance for an education, and travels with his
relative to Boston.
ISBN 0-688-15670-3
[1. Frontier and pioneer life—Fiction.   2. Voyages and travels—
Fiction.   3. Uncles—Fiction.]   I. Dodson, Bert, ill.   II. Title.   III. Series:
Pryor, Bonnie.   American adventures.
PZ7.P94965Lu 1999   [Fic]—DC21   98-47498   CIP   AC

Contents

AMERICAN ADVENTURES

Luke

ONE

————— • —————

A Rescue

Luke Reed gave the reins a gentle pull. "Whoa, Jack." The big black horse pulling the plow stood obediently while Luke slipped out of the harness and waited for his father to catch up.

"Your mother thought you'd be hungry by now," Mr. Reed said, handing him a basket. "I'll take over for a while." He looked approvingly at the thin dark lines cutting through the prairie sod. "You've done a lot."

"Jack has been acting up the last few rows,"

Luke said. "Don't know what's the matter with him."

Mr. Reed checked the harness to make sure it wasn't rubbing. "Everything looks all right," he said, scratching behind Jack's ears. "Maybe Jack would rather be in the nice shady barn," he joked, looking up at the hot Iowa sun.

Jack gave a loud snort. His eyes showed a bit of white. "He does seem a little nervous," Mr. Reed said thoughtfully. "Maybe there's a snake nearby."

As Luke looked at his bare feet and shuddered, Mr. Reed chuckled. "Snakes are more afraid of you than you are of them."

"Ha," Luke said. "I don't bite."

Mr. Reed adjusted the harness and slapped the reins. "Gee!" Jack started forward, and Mr. Reed guided the plow in a narrow straight line. Luke checked the ground before he sank down in the tall grass and opened the basket. His mother had packed fresh bread and a hunk of cheese. There was also a small jug of cool milk and a piece of apple cake wrapped up in a cloth napkin. Luke quickly gobbled down the food. He had been workly morning, and his stomach was

 father at the plow, wishing he
 nd charcoal. He imagined how
the picture would look when he was finished—
Jack, strong and sleek, and the prairie grass stretch-
ing endlessly. Luke sighed. His father did not
understand Luke's desire to turn everything he
saw into a picture. Mr. Reed thought drawing was
a waste of time.

His father reached the end of the field and was
heading back on the next row. The tall grass
formed a thick mat of roots, making it impossible
to plow. This was called sod. Cutting the sod was
only the first step in preparing the prairie for
planting. After this first cut the sod would be
turned over and left to rot for a year. The second
year they would plow, but still the land would not
be good enough for most crops. His father would
plant flax, a crop that could be grown in poor soil.

Some farmers hired crews for the backbreaking
work of cutting and turning over the sod, but Mr.
Reed had done it all alone with only the help of

Luke and his younger brothers. "The crews charge two dollars an acre," he'd explained to Luke. "That's more than the land itself cost."

Even without help Mr. Reed was slowly winning the battle against the prairie. This year nearly forty acres were planted in corn, another twenty in flax, and ten more were newly cut.

Luke finished his lunch and stretched out on the ground, easing his tired muscles. The sun beat down, and he closed his eyes against the brightness. He wished there were a tree somewhere, so he could sit in its shade. There were trees in Ohio, where they had lived before. He could barely remember them, but when he drifted off to sleep, he dreamed of their leafy coolness.

A sudden shout from his father brought him awake. He jumped to his feet, bewildered for a minute by his sleep-fogged mind.

Across the field he could see Jack rearing in the air and his father fighting to hold him. A terrible sound came from Jack, a sound more like a scream than a noise a horse should ever make. Luke stood frozen in confusion.

A black cloud seemed to surround his father and

Jack. His father had dropped the plow and was reaching to free himself from the harness. Suddenly Jack bolted and raced across the field toward Luke. Mr. Reed, still caught in the harness, was thrown to the ground. He cried out in agony as he was dragged along with the plow across the field. The black cloud seemed to follow.

Luke was sick with fear, but even so he found himself moving. The angry buzz of bees reached his ears, and he realized what had happened. The plow had cut through a nest of them hidden in the tall prairie grass.

"Whoa, Jack," Luke screamed as he frantically tried to reach the wildly frightened horse. He felt a sting on his arm and then another, but intent on stopping Jack before the horse swerved away, he raced into the swarm. Jack pounded toward him, and Luke feared he would be crushed beneath the horse's giant hooves. He knew he would have only one chance to grab the harness. If he missed it, his father would dragged to his death across the prairie.

Normally Jack was gentle, but now he was so spooked that his eyes rolled back and foamy sweat ran down his sides. The plow bounced wildly, coming dangerously close to Mr. Reed, who was still slamming helplessly on the ground with every beat of Jack's hooves.

Luke braced himself, ready to grab the harness. Then at the last second Jack turned. Luke made a desperate lunge.

"Whoa, Jack!" he shouted again. For an instant he thought he had missed, but then his fingers closed around the leather harness. Jack was still straining to break free. Luke's fingers felt as if they were being ripped from his hands as he fought with every ounce of strength to hold on.

It was enough to give Mr. Reed a chance to roll free. For a moment Luke and the horse seemed suspended in time. The hair on Jack's back glistened in sweat. The bees had spent their fury and were disappearing back into the ground with only a few buzzing stragglers to show they had ever been there.

Jack let out a whoosh of air and stopped struggling. Luke slowly released his hold on the harness. The horse walked a few steps away and then stopped. His head hung and his sides heaved as he gasped for air.

Mr. Reed remained on the ground, not moving. Fearful that his father was seriously injured, Luke stumbled over to him. He saw angry red welts on his father's face and arms.

With a groan Mr. Reed sat up. He felt his arms and legs as though checking for wounds. Dark bruises were forming between the stings.

"Nothing seems to be broken. I guess Jack knew more than we did," he said finally. Slowly and painfully he stood up, swaying slightly. His face and arms were swelling, but he waved his arm toward Jack. "Unhook the plow and walk Jack back. If we don't cool him off, he'll get sick."

Luke did as his father said, all the time watching him out of the corner of his eye. Too weak to stand, Mr. Reed sank down on the ground. "You'll have to ride Jack," said Luke, suddenly in charge.

Mr. Reed nodded. He allowed Luke to help him up and, using Luke's bent knee, managed to get up on Jack's broad back. Luke led the horse, walking as fast as he dared across the fields until they were close to the sod house.

His brothers, Caleb and Michael, saw him before he could call out. They ran into the house, and a second later Mrs. Reed appeared holding Nellie, their baby sister. She handed the baby to Caleb and raced out to meet them.

"My stars! What has happened?" she asked.

"Luke saved my life," Mr. Reed mumbled through swollen lips.

Luke and his brothers helped Mrs. Reed get their father into the house and onto the bed. While she treated her husband's wounds and covered the stings with a salve, Luke sat down at the table and allowed himself finally to relax. Now that it was all over, he was surprised to find that his legs were shaking.

"Jack," he said, suddenly remembering the horse.

Usually Caleb would have argued if Luke had told him to do something. Now he looked at Luke with a new kind of respect. Luke was glad they didn't know how frightened he'd been. "Michael and I will take care of Jack," Caleb said.

Mrs. Reed bustled by with a pan of water to wash Mr. Reed's wounds. "Rub some of this salve on Jack's stings," she said, handing Caleb a jar.

Luke rested his arms on the table and put his head down. Caleb and Michael headed outside just as their twin sisters, Mary Alice and Catherine Louise, burst through the door. They had been playing in the barn. "What happened?" they clamored together.

Luke did not answer. As soon as his eyes had closed, he had fallen sound asleep.

TWO

— ❖ —

The Peddler

The stings and scrapes healed quickly, and Mr. Reed was able to go back to work in less than a week. One afternoon the twins were playing with their cornstalk dolls on the roof of the sod house when they saw a wagon pulled by two strong black mules.

"Thumbody's coming," they shouted together, through identical missing front teeth. They slid down the side of the roof, loosing a shower of dirt from the ceiling inside. It fell onto the table, where Luke was sitting, and sprinkled over his last piece of drawing paper. Without thinking he brushed at the dirt, smearing his charcoal drawing.

"Tarnation," he yelled, jumping up from his chair and knocking it over.

Startled by the crash of the chair, his mother looked up from her mending. "Luke!" she said sharply. Then her face softened as she looked with sympathy at his ruined picture. "You've been working so hard on it."

Luke righted the chair. He looked at his picture and frowned. "It doesn't matter. The nose wasn't right. I can never make the noses look right."

The twins burst through the door. "It's the—," began Mary Alice. "Peddler," finished Catherine Louise.

Luke had opened his mouth to yell at the girls, but with the news he forgot all his anger. It had been several weeks since they had had a visitor of any sort, but there was no one Luke wanted to see more than Rufus Tansy, the peddler.

He stepped outside and shaded his eyes from the bright sun. Even without the vantage of the sod house roof he could see the thin cloud of dust as the peddler's wagon moved slowly down the road.

The peddler was still a long way off, but the prairie was so flat that Luke could see for miles.

"Fetch some cool water from the well," Mrs. Reed said briskly. "Mr. Tansy will be thirsty after all that dust."

Luke took the wooden lid off the well and lowered the bucket. Then he filled the watering trough for the two long-eared mules Rufus called his ladies. They would be thirsty too.

The wagon had nearly reached the house when Mr. Reed and Caleb and Michael came in from the field where they had been repairing a fence. The boys were poking each other and laughing. Caleb and Michael were so ornery that Mr. Reed claimed he had to keep them busy to keep them out of mischief.

The family lined up to wait while Rufus reined in the mules and stepped down. First was Mr. Reed, who was tall and rather stern-appearing, although he was almost always gentle with his family. Beside him stood Mrs. Reed, plump and usually cheerful. Mrs. Reed held Nellie, who was just starting to crawl, while the twins, seven years old and looking so much alike that even Luke could not always tell them apart, stood next to their mother. Then came Michael, who was eight and had red hair and freckles like his mother. Caleb was nine, two years younger than Luke. His hair was dark like Luke's and their father's, but his eyes were blue. Luke stood last in line. He looked out the corner of his eye at the rest of his family, trying to see them as the peddler might. Someday he would paint them all just like this, all in a row. If only he could learn how to make noses correctly!

"Hello, Reeds," Rufus called out in his booming voice. Luke ran over to offer the water and put the bucket down for the dusty mules.

"My ladies are mighty glad to get that water," Rufus Tansy said. "Half the streams we passed were dried up."

He took a giant handkerchief out of his pocket and mopped at his brow. "Hot," he remarked. He peered up at the sky, blue and cloudless. "Sure need some rain. At least you still have your well," he said, tipping up the dipper for the last drop. "Last farm I was at had their well run dry. Nothing but dust."

"It's been a dry spring, all right," said Mr. Reed.

"Our well is good and deep," he added, "but we're worried about the corn." He waved his arm at the field, at the new growth already stunted and brown.

Luke fidgeted, waiting for the pleasantries to end. He hoped the peddler would give some sign that he remembered Luke's request. He had made it when Tansy visited just before the winter snows had started. Now it was nearly May. The peddler did not look his way as he spread a blanket under a tree and began laying out his wares. Luke's heart sank. Had he forgotten?

The twins were already inching closer to see. Luke looked at the goods spread out on the blanket. There were spices and sewing needles, bars of company soap that smelled like roses. There were knives and a shiny new hatchet. Mr. Reed looked at the hatchet for a long time before laying it back down. Luke looked at everything, but he didn't spot the box of crayons he had asked for. Rufus must have forgotten.

After Mr. and Mrs. Reed selected their purchases, the peddler sat down to tell them all the news and latest gossip. Mrs. McKay's baby had died, and Mr. Johnson's new horse had stepped in a prairie dog hole and broken its leg.

"Settled the war with Mexico too," Rufus informed them. "We got a whole big new parcel of land out west. Just in time, I suppose. There's rumors someone's found gold out in California."

"Gold?" Mr. Reed asked.

Rufus shrugged. "Might be just rumors, but that's what folks are saying."

Mrs. Reed and the girls went inside to prepare the evening meal. "Supper will be ready in a few minutes," Mrs. Reed announced from the doorway. "You'll stay, won't you, Mr. Tansy?"

"Thank you kindly," Rufus Tansy said. "I'm always glad to get a good home-cooked supper." Suddenly he looked at Luke. "I almost forgot. We have a special bit of trading." The peddler reached under the wagon seat and handed Luke a package wrapped in brown paper. Eagerly Luke ripped it open. Inside were a small tin with brightly colored crayons, and a stack of smooth white paper. The crayons were wrapped in paper so they could be held like pencils. Lovingly Luke touched the bright colors, imagining the pictures he could draw. Here were a blue nearly like the sky on a summer day and a red like the Indian paintbrush that dotted the prairie in the spring.

"What is it? What is it?" Caleb and Michael crowded in for a look. Their faces fell when they saw the crayons.

"I thought you were getting something good," Caleb said.

"Like a pearl-handled knife," said Michael. "That's what I'd get."

Mr. Reed frowned when he saw the crayons.

"I won't draw until my chores are done," Luke promised.

"Still a waste of a good trade," Mr. Reed said sourly. "There's plenty of things we need."

Rufus unexpectedly took his side. "Maybe Luke here will grow up to be a famous artist."

"Pictures don't feed a family," Mr. Reed grumped. But he left Luke and Rufus alone to do their bargaining.

Luke ran to a small storage shed and returned with a stack of furs. "I trapped these myself last winter," he said proudly.

Rufus fingered the pelts. "Not as much market

for these as there once was. Still, I imagine I can sell them. You've made yourself a bargain."

After supper Rufus told them more about the gold. "Some fellow found a whole lot of it at a place called Sutter's Mill," he said. "Some folks say it's just lying on the ground, waiting for a body to pick it up. Others think it was just a lucky find. No one knows for sure. I suppose a lot of fools will go rushing out west now."

Mr. Reed frowned at such foolishness. "I couldn't go if I wanted. Got a crop to get in. Planning on starting the house this fall too."

Luke's mother smiled. "It will be wonderful to be in a real house again. The only good thing I can say about sod houses is that they are cool in the summer."

"Well, you've made this one right comfortable," Rufus said.

Luke looked around the house, trying to see it as a stranger might. There was only one big room. The rag rugs his mother had woven covered the dirt floor. His father had hung a canvas sheet to separate the sleeping area into two small rooms, one for the parents and one for Luke and his brothers and sisters. His mother had painted the sod walls with whitewash, and although bits of the brown earth showed through here and there, the whitewash brightened the room. In one corner his mother had hung several of Luke's drawings. The sod house was cool in the summer and warm when the winter winds blew. In spite of the occasional dirt and bugs that fell from the roof, everything was clean and neat.

Suddenly he realized his father was talking about him. "If it wasn't for my son here, I wouldn't be speaking to you," he declared.

Luke felt his face grow hot. "Wasn't much," he said modestly. "Just reached out and caught Jack."

Inwardly Luke groaned. Rufus Tansy would be carrying that story all over the territory. He excused himself and went outside. He was anxious to try out his new crayons, but he'd promised Caleb and Michael he would play a game of baseball now that it was cooler outside. Even though they didn't have enough people for a real game, they enjoyed playing. Uncle Eli had taught them on one of his visits. Sometimes they even talked their parents into joining in. Tonight, however, their parents stayed in the house, catching up on the news. When they trooped in later, tired, dusty, and ready for bed, Rufus Tansy was still sitting at the table, talking. He spent the night, sleeping in the barn with his ladies, even though Mrs. Reed offered to make him up a bed in the house.

It was late morning when the peddler finally hitched his mules back to his wagon. "My ladies are mighty fidgety today," he remarked as he climbed up in the wagon. "Guess they are anxious to get going. I'll see you in a few months." With a wave he rolled away, heading west.

Mr. Reed put on the battered old straw hat he wore to keep off the sun. "It's always nice to have some company," he said, "but chores are late. Let's get back to work."

THREE

A Sudden Storm

It was nearly suppertime when Luke finished the last of his chores and gratefully walked back into the earthy but cooler air of the house. He flopped down on a rag rug, moaning with relief.

"My stars, Luke, how can I fix supper with you lying in the middle of the floor?" Mrs. Reed asked good-naturedly.

"It is too hot to eat anyway," Luke remarked.

Mrs. Reed chuckled. "You say that now. But when your stomach starts rumbling, you'll change your tune. Now shoo." She shook her apron at him as if he were a wayward chicken she was chasing back to the coop. In spite of her scolding, she was smiling.

"Would you like some help?" he asked, looking for an excuse to stay in the cool house.

Mrs. Reed hesitated. "We are nearly out of butter."

Luke groaned. Making butter was not his favorite thing to do, but at least it would keep him indoors. He checked the cream, which was in a pan on the table. Mrs. Reed had let it sit out all day, and now it was shiny and smelled slightly sour, perfect for making butter. He poured it into the wooden churn and sat down on a high stool, then pounded the paddle up and down, up and down. Through the open door he watched the twins as he worked. They were sitting by the cottonwood trees Mr. Reed had planted when the family first moved to the prairie. One of the twins' chores was to carry a bucket of water to the trees every day, and because of the care the trees were shooting up fast. They had not grown big enough to shade the sod house, but they looked nice. The twins were playing with a dollhouse Mr. Reed had made for them last winter.

Michael raced into the house and, reaching into a pouch he carried, slyly showed Luke a small black snake. Then he joined Caleb outside.

As Michael and Caleb approached, the twins put their arms protectively around the dollhouse. "Get away," they ordered.

Michael looked innocent. "We're not going to bother you. We just wanted to give you something."

The twins were suspicious. They were used to their brothers' tricks. "What?" they asked in unison.

"This!" shouted Michael. He dropped the snake in the dollhouse.

Shrieking, the twins jumped up and chased their brothers. The boys ran just fast enough to let the girls almost catch them; then they would put on a burst of speed.

Luke laughed out loud watching them. Nearly half an hour had passed, and the cream was starting to feel heavy. He peeked into the churn and saw that the milk had separated into buttermilk and fat globs of butter. He poured off the buttermilk, to be used for baking. Then his mother gathered the butter into a bowl and rinsed it several times with water. She squeezed out the last of the rinse water and sprinkled the ball of butter with salt to keep it from spoiling. Some she put on the table for supper. The rest she pressed into a crock, which she handed to Luke. "Take this to the fruit cellar," she said.

The fruit cellar was a few yards away at the spot Mr. Reed had chosen for the new house. Two wooden doors opened to reveal a ramp leading down under the ground. The cellar was a cool dark place to store meats, vegetables, and fruits.

When Luke walked outside, his father was coming in for supper. The weather had changed while Luke had been making the butter. The air had been heavy and still, but now dark clouds scurried across the sky and distant lightning lit the horizon.

"At last!" Mr. Reed exclaimed.

Luke grinned happily. He sprinted the distance to the cellar, pulled open the doors and hurried down the ramp into the cool underground. Along the stone-lined walls, Mr. Reed had fitted some shelves. Several barrels on the floor contained the last of the supplies from winter—molasses, salt, and dried apples packed in layers of straw. Luke covered the bowl of butter with a cloth and set it on the nearest shelf.

By the time he secured the cellar doors, the storm had moved almost directly overhead. An angry zigzag lit up the sky, and thunder cracked loudly enough to rattle the doors. Luke streaked back to the house. The first few drops of rain spotted his shirt.

"Let's eat," said Mrs. Reed. She set candles on the table. Even though Mr. Reed had fitted two tiny windows of real glass in the sod house, the storm had turned early evening into night.

"Dinner smells good," Mr. Reed told his wife.

Mrs. Reed had stewed a rooster from her flock. Michael and Caleb smacked their lips. "This is the first good thing that old rooster ever did," Caleb said.

The rooster had been a mean bird, with a habit of pecking anyone who walked by, but he tasted delicious cooked up in a stew with biscuits on top.

Michael pointed to the ceiling. "We're getting a leak."

A dark stain was spreading above them. Mrs. Reed sighed as she put a wooden bowl out to catch the muddy drips. Then another drip started. She looked at the roof in dismay.

Mr. Reed stood up and picked up his plate. "A little rain shouldn't spoil such a good dinner. The table will be a good umbrella for a picnic."

They all grabbed their plates and squeezed under the table, where it was dry. Mr. Reed looked at his wife and smiled. "It won't be like this forever. Maybe by fall we can start work on the new house," he said. Mr. Reed had told them that the house would have real wood floors and a roof that wouldn't leak.

The twins clapped their hands. "No more bugs!" they shouted together.

Caleb gave them a wicked smile. "Don't worry. I'll still find them for you."

Everyone laughed. Mrs. Reed stacked the dishes

for washing. "It's neighbors I would like the most," she said softly. "Another woman to talk to now and then."

"Someday you'll have those too," answered Mr. Reed. "More people are coming every day."

The twins looked out one of the windows. "It's stopped," began Mary Alice. "Raining," finished Catherine Louise.

Luke opened the door. Usually a rain cleared the air and made it cooler. This time it seemed even hotter, and the sky was still threatening and dark.

His father stood beside him at the door. "Not enough rain." He sighed.

"Maybe we'll get more," Luke said, pointing to the sky. "It still looks stormy."

Mr. Reed nodded. He managed to look discouraged yet hopeful at the same time. "It might at that."

A sudden wind came up, blowing through the grass in the fields his father had not yet plowed.

"Don't you ever get tired of this place?" Luke asked suddenly.

Mr. Reed looked surprised. "Tired of our farm?"

Luke fumbled to explain. "All the work, fighting the weather all the time." He waved his arm at the flat prairie. "The sameness."

"I don't mind the work," Mr. Reed said sharply. "In Ohio I worked twelve hours a day for another man. It took years to save the money for this land. Now I work even harder, but it's for the dream your mother and I share—a fine house and fields of crops and land that is ours for as far—" Mr. Reed broke off in frustration. "You're my oldest son. I hoped you would share that dream."

"I have a dream of my own," Luke said hesitantly.

Mr. Reed gave an angry snort. "To draw pretty pictures? That's a foolish dream, a child's dream. It's time to put away such a silly notion."

Luke's jaw clenched, but he did not answer. Sighing, his father turned away. Luke went to his room. Before he went to bed, he took out the box of crayons from the small chest where he kept his belongings and once again admired the beautiful colors.

Luke thought about the first time he had realized he wanted to be an artist. He had not been much older than the twins, he remembered. He had been sitting in the dirt, trying to draw the tanner's horse, when his uncle Eli stopped to watch. "Try this," Uncle Eli had said, adding a few lines with another stick.

Uncle Eli had gone to Boston as a young man and had become quite rich buying and selling goods. He was like Rufus Tansy, Luke thought. Except that Rufus was content to sell his goods from farm to farm while Uncle Eli took whole wagon trains full of goods along the Santa Fe Trail, returning each time with his pockets full of silver and more goods to sell in Boston.

The next time Uncle Eli visited, he'd brought a tablet of paper and several real pencils. Luke still remembered the thrill when he'd finished his first picture using them.

Luke put away his crayons and stretched out on the bed he shared with Caleb and Michael. It was too sticky to sleep, and he tossed restlessly. He was envious of his brothers' ability to fall asleep quickly. Suddenly he sat straight up.

There was a clattering sound outside. Although the mud bricks muffled the sound, he could hear the pings of ice hitting the little window. "Hail," he muttered, jumping out of bed.

FOUR

———•———

Town

By daylight the hail had melted, but the devastation it left behind was plain. The hailstones had been small at first, but they grew larger. Chunks of ice had crashed against the windows until the family feared the glass would break. As soon as it was light enough to see, Luke followed his father to the fields. They stood silently, surveying the damage. The ice had cut and crushed the tender cornstalks. There was hardly a plant that wasn't damaged.

Mr. Reed straightened his shoulders. "Let Caleb and Michael take care of the milking. Luke, you hitch up Jack and Maud. There still might be time to get in a new crop. We'll go into town for more seed. There's money for some, and perhaps Mr. Kline will give us credit for the rest."

Although Luke was often forgetful when it came to his chores and clumsy when it came to building and repairs, he had a special way with animals. Maud and Jack stood quietly while he hitched them to the wagon. When he was done, he checked to make sure the lines did not rub. Like Mr. Reed, Jack had healed quickly. He snuffled at the leather pouch around Luke's neck. Reaching in, Luke pulled out a handful of grain. He offered some to both horses, holding his hand straight so he wasn't bitten when Jack scooped up the grain with his big teeth.

Mrs. Reed came outside with a basket packed with bread, cheese, and a jug of cool water.

"We'll be back by dark," Mr. Reed told her slapping the reins. The horses took off at a brisk trot, and Luke settled down for the long ride.

The deeply rutted road to Georgetown was already dry. Tall prairie grass grew on both sides of the road, making it seem almost like a tunnel. After a time Mr. Reed handed the reins to Luke. The horses plodded on, mile after mile. There was little conversation. At last they began to pass a few scattered farms, and finally they reached the town itself.

"Look at that," Mr. Reed said, pointing to the houses. "How can people live all cramped up together like that?"

Luke rather liked the town. He marveled at the houses, mostly sturdy two stories built right next to one another on tree-lined roads. He envied the children who played in some of the yards. It made him wonder if town kids ever had chores to do.

The businesses were lined up along the main street. They passed a bank, a blacksmith and livery stable, a small hotel that served as a stagecoach stop, a restaurant, and a saloon—plus two churches with tall white steeples. Next to one of the churches was a doctor's office, and then came Mr. Kline's general store. Even though it was small, Georgetown was usually bustling. People hurried along the wooden sidewalks, and horses and wagons were tied in front of every shop. Luke could never understand what the townspeople did all day to look so busy.

Mr. Reed tied Maud and Jack to the rail in front of Mr. Kline's store. Two old men were sitting at a table just inside the door, playing cards. One of them spat out a chunk of tobacco. It went through the open door and landed on the wooden sidewalk.

"My corn is going to have to be replanted," Mr. Reed told Mr. Kline as they entered the store.

The storekeeper nodded. "You're not the first this morning," he said.

"Can I walk around some?" Luke asked.

Mr. Reed nodded. "Don't go too far. My business won't take that long."

Luke walked down the street. When he turned the corner, he passed a ladies' hat shop. Fancy hats were displayed on posts in the window. There was a blue one with tiny white flowers in the front. His mother would look nice in a hat like that.

He was so busy thinking about the hat that he didn't notice the two boys until they were standing beside him. "Look here," one of them said. "The soddy boy wants a new hat."

The second boy snickered. "Maybe you want to look in the dress shop too."

Luke clenched his hands into a fist as he turned to face his tormentors. "I was looking at it for my mother."

The first boy was a head taller than Luke. He leaned forward until his nose almost touched Luke's. "I thought you were looking at it for yourself. Anyhow, a hat like that is for a lady, not some old soddy woman."

Without thinking, Luke swung his fists. The boy yelped and fell back, holding his nose. A little trickle of blood ran through his fingers.

Before Luke could think, the other boy jumped on him, pounding him with his fists. The two fell on the dusty street and rolled over and over. Then the first boy jumped back into the fracas, and Luke felt blows everywhere.

Suddenly Luke felt the weight being lifted off him. He peeked through already swelling eyes to see a man holding on to both boys.

The town boys were sputtering. "He started it," one of them whined.

Luke scrambled to his feet. "Uncle Eli," he cried happily, forgetting about his bruises and scrapes. He shook his head to clear it.

"He hit me first," the same boy complained, struggling to get free.

Uncle Eli didn't loosen his grip. "Is that true?" he asked Luke.

Slowly Luke nodded. "I didn't like something he said," he explained.

Uncle Eli gave the boys a shake and released them. "Still, was two against one. Don't seem too fair to me."

With a final glare at Luke the boys ran off. Luke gingerly touched his eye.

"Your mama's not going to be happy with you." Uncle Eli chuckled. "Maybe you need to think before you punch. What do you care what those two say?"

"They were saying something mean about Mama," Luke said.

Uncle Eli laughed. "I probably would've done

the same thing when I was your age. Come on. I'll walk with you in case those two get any ideas about an ambush. Is your dad at Mr. Kline's store?"

Luke nodded. "He's going to be surprised to see you."

"Didn't he get my letter?"

Luke shook his head. "This is the first time we've been to town in over a month."

The same two old men were still sitting by the door. "Looks like you walked into a brick wall," one of them cackled.

Mr. Reed came out carrying several bags of seed. "What happened to you?" he asked Luke. Then he saw Uncle Eli. He dropped the bag into the wagon, and the two brothers hugged.

Just then Mr. Kline came out of the store. "Oh, I almost forgot," he said. "You have a letter. Came a couple of weeks ago. There's thirty cents' postage due."

"Throw it away," Uncle Eli said. "It's old news now."

Mr. Kline looked annoyed. Luke knew he always made some extra money when the mail came, reading it to people who could not read. His father was one of those people.

Mr. Kline looked at Luke. "I'm in need of an extra hand. Luke here would do just fine. He could board with my family and maybe even attend school when he's not working. It'd be good if someone in your family learned to read."

"I need him on the farm," Mr. Reed said, bristling.

"I meant in the winter, when there is not so much to do."

"Thank you for the offer," Mr. Reed said curtly. "But I need him at home."

Luke gave his father a grateful look. He didn't like Mr. Kline. Once he had heard the storekeeper talking about the "soddies" with a sneer in his voice, and another time he had seen him beating a hired boy with a stick.

He followed his father and uncle back to the wagon. Eli had been traveling east through the Kansas territories. "I had a buyer for some horses, so I came north with a few of my men," he said. "They're getting a wheel repaired at the blacksmith's. Soon as I can get the drivers on their way back to Boston, I'll come visit for a few days."

Mr. Reed slapped the reins on the horses' backs. "See you soon," Luke called as they started the slow, bumpy ride back home.

FIVE

Uncle Eli

Caleb and Michael were as excited as Luke. A visit from Uncle Eli was fun for everyone. He always had stories to tell of the Santa Fe Trail. Sometimes his wagon trains were even attacked by Indians. "When is he coming? Does he look the same?" they clamored.

Finally Mr. Reed threw up his hands and laughed. "You'd think the president was coming."

Mrs. Reed looked around the sod house. "Maybe we could fix up the house a little before he comes."

Mr. Reed laughed again. "Figured you'd say that. I got an extra sack of lime."

Luke wrinkled his nose. One of his least favorite jobs was putting a scoop of lime down the holes in the outhouse each week. But that same lime, mixed with water and salt, made the whitewash that kept the walls of the little house looking so clean and bright.

Luke helped his father replant the corn. Every day he watched the road for some sign of Uncle Eli, but the days rolled by, and he didn't come. With the help of a rainy day new green shoots were soon breaking through. Mr. Reed was so pleased that he didn't even complain when he saw Luke with his paints.

Then long days went by without another rainfall. Mr. Reed watched the sky with a worried frown, but it remained blue and cloudless, and the sun unusually hot. When the wind blew, dust filled the air, making everyone's mouth feel gritty. June passed, and then it was July. The only living things that seemed to enjoy this weather were the flies. They clung to the cows in black clouds, making them twitchy and irritable when they were milked. Even though it made the house stuffy, Mrs. Reed insisted that the door be kept closed to keep insects out.

It had been well over a month since they had seen Uncle Eli, and Luke had stopped watching for him. Then one day, as he headed back to the house with the morning milk, he saw a rider in the distance. The man was alone, but he was leading a second horse loaded down with supplies.

Luke put down the heavy buckets and ran inside. "Someone's coming," he yelled.

Mrs. Reed came to the door and shaded her eyes to see. "I think it's Eli. Go fetch your father," she told the twins.

"Uncle Eli, Uncle Eli," they shouted as they raced to the pasture. Mr. Reed was there, preparing to cut more sod. He made it back to the house just as Uncle Eli rode up the lane from the road. By the time Uncle Eli reached the house, Luke had filled the trough with fresh water.

"My horses are mighty dry," Uncle Eli said, handing Luke the reins. The horse he was riding was a beautiful roan. She pranced nervously when Luke brought her a bucket of oats.

"I call her Beauty," Uncle Eli said, noticing Luke's admiring looks. "And the packhorse here is Donovan."

"I can see why you named her Beauty," Luke said, patting the horse's flank.

"Maybe I'll let you ride her sometime," Uncle Eli said. His eyes crinkled under the layers of dust.

"Luke has a good hand with horses," Mr. Reed said.

Luke felt a warm glow at his father's words. He wasn't a man who gave compliments lightly.

"Supper will be ready soon," Mrs. Reed said. "I expect you're hungry."

"What I am is dirty," Uncle Eli said. "I see things are still mighty dry around here. Can you spare enough water for a bath?"

Mr. Reed carried the big tub to the back of the house, and his wife heated water in a big kettle and poured it into the tub. She handed Uncle Eli a bar of company soap she'd bought the month before from Rufus Tansy. It was smoother and better-smelling than the soap she made at home. Uncle Eli sniffed it and winked at Luke. "I'll smell like a bouquet of roses after this."

The Reed family went into the house to wait. A minute later Mrs. Reed said, "My stars, what is that noise?"

In a very loud and slightly off-key voice Uncle Eli was singing.

"Buffalo gals, won't you come out tonight,
Come out tonight, come out tonight.
Buffalo gals, won't you come out tonight,
Annnnnnnnd dance by the light of the moon."

The twins giggled and covered their ears. Mrs. Reed just shook her head. "My stars," she said again.

Mrs. Reed was just setting a meal of fried pork, boiled potatoes, and corn bread on the table when Uncle Eli came into the house. He looked like a different person with his hair clean and his beard neatly trimmed. It was plain to see he was Mr. Reed's brother. Both had dark hair and the same color brown eyes, but Uncle Eli's face was more crinkled with laugh lines.

"I feel better," he announced. "I'm carrying quite a bit of money with me. A person is smart not to look too prosperous riding across the prairie by himself."

"What took you so long to get here?" Luke blurted out.

"My crews all deserted me. Wanted to head to California with the rest of the country. I talked them into taking the wagons to Independence at least. I figured I'd better go with them, make sure they got there. My partners are going to try to sell everything in Independence. I promised to rejoin them there in a couple of weeks. Independence is a real boomtown. Seems like half the people are heading west. Everyone is hoping to get rich."

Mr. Reed shook his head. "Foolishness. Working the land is where the riches are."

"How long can you stay, Uncle Eli?" Luke asked.

Mr. Reed frowned at him for interrupting grown-up conversation, but Uncle Eli answered, "About a week if you can put up with me that long."

After supper Uncle Eli told them about his last trip. "The Spanish settlers in Santa Fe are eager for goods," he said. "My partners and I took fifteen thousand dollars' worth of goods there, and we came back with seventy-five thousand dollars' worth of silver and trade wares."

"Will you be making more trips to Santa Fe?" asked Mrs. Reed.

"I think this will be my last one," Uncle Eli told them. "Indians are getting riled up at all the white folks crossing their land. Some folks are heading for the Oregon Territory. And the rest to California. Actually I've been thinking about heading to California myself. All those people out there are going to need building and mining supplies. I figure I could get a lot of that gold and not have to dig for it."

"Do you think they are really finding gold?" asked Mr. Reed.

Uncle Eli shook his head no. "I suspect it is greatly overtold. There's a fellow named Henry Simpson who's written a guidebook called *Three Weeks in a Gold Mine*. It costs twelve and a half cents. Twenty-five if you want a map. Most people are treating it like gospel, but I think it's a fake. I think Henry Simpson has never been to the gold mines. His gold mine is selling that book to fools."

"So you think it is all lies?" Mr. Reed asked.

Uncle Eli shook his head. "May be some truth. I don't know."

Michael forgot his manners. "What is gold?"

Mr. Reed frowned, but Uncle Eli smiled. "It's a little yellow rock that makes people go crazy," he said.

Making a scary face, he chased Michael and Caleb out of the house and around the barn. Luke stood outside the door, listening to the peals of laughter from his brothers. Uncle Eli was the kind of person who made you feel good just to be near. Even his father was smiling and relaxed. Luke found himself wishing that Uncle Eli would stay forever.

SIX

Prairie Days

The next afternoon Luke worked on a drawing of Beauty. Uncle Eli had turned her out in the pasture with the other horses. Donovan, the packhorse, settled in right away with the Reeds' two horses, but Beauty was another story. Jack and Maud huddled together, as though they were not sure what to make of the newcomer romping and kicking in the prairie grass. Beauty was like Uncle Eli, Luke thought as he drew. His father was more like Jack, steady and hardworking.

"That's wonderful," Uncle Eli said. Luke had

been so intent on his drawing he had not heard him approach.

Luke held the picture up and looked at it critically. "Do you think so? I'm having trouble getting her legs just right."

"That's the best drawing I've ever seen," Uncle Eli said. "It's as good as some I've seen in fancy art galleries back east. I like to draw some myself, but I don't have the feel for it that you do."

"It's nice to have something new to draw. I can only draw what I see," Luke admitted. "Not much new around here. I wish I'd seen all those things you talk about. I'd like to draw mountains and Indians and the wagon trains heading west."

"I don't imagine my brother understands all this."

Luke shook his head no. "He thinks it's a waste of time. He says I'll never be able to make a living drawing pictures."

"He might be right," Uncle Eli said. He looked suddenly thoughtful. "Do you go to school?"

Again Luke shook his head no. "The nearest school is at Georgetown, and that's half a day away. Besides, Papa needs me at home."

"Then you can't read?"

"I went to first grade in Ohio," said Luke, "but I've forgotten most of it. Not much use for book learning working on a farm."

Uncle Eli looked around toward the horizon. "This is a fine place. I can see why Jeremiah loves it so. But there's an awful lot of world out there. A man needs to read if he's going to make his way. Best thing I ever did, learning how to read and write."

"How did you learn?" Luke asked.

"Well, I wasn't much older than you when I was apprenticed to a silversmith. I lived in his house, and in the evenings he taught me. Your father went to the mill when he was ten. He never got the chance to learn." Uncle Eli hesitated. "Would you like me to teach you?"

"Do you think I could learn?" Luke asked.

"Course you can. There's nothing to it. Do you remember the alphabet?"

Luke shrugged. "Some."

"Reading is just learning how to put that alphabet together to make words." With a stick he scratched something in the dirt. "This is your name," he explained.

Luke looked at the strange shapes in the dirt. He took the stick and copied the letters underneath Uncle Eli's. "Perfect!" his uncle exclaimed. "I guess it's because you're an artist."

Luke felt a warm glow. Uncle Eli had called him an artist. Eagerly he scratched out the letters again.

Luke's father walked across the field toward them. "What's this?" he asked, frowning at the letters in the dirt.

"Uncle Eli taught me how to write my name!" Luke exclaimed.

"The boy should be going to school," Uncle Eli said.

"Don't go putting notions in his head," Mr. Reed said.

"Too bad Luke can't come back to Boston with me," Uncle Eli said thoughtfully. "I could teach him my business and see that he got an education."

"He's too young to know what he wants," Mr. Reed said shortly, "and I need him here."

"Well, at least let me begin to teach him while

I'm visiting," Uncle Eli said. "I could teach all the young 'uns."

Mr. Reed shrugged. "I guess it can't do any harm. But don't go neglecting your chores," he added to Luke.

Catherine Louise ran up to their uncle and tugged on his arm. "Uncle Eli, you promised to come to our tea party."

Mary Alice tugged at the other arm. "It's all ready," she said.

"Be careful," Luke warned. "Last time they talked me into one of those tea parties, they gave me a buffalo dropping and said it was cake."

With a grin over his shoulder Uncle Eli followed the twins. His cheerful off-key voice trailed back,

> "Jimmy crack corn and I don't care,
> Jimmy crack corn and I don't care,
> Jimmy crack corn and I don't care,
> My master's gone away."

There wasn't much chance for lessons the next day. Luke spent all his time cleaning the barn. He put down clean straw for the four lambs. Mrs. Reed was hoping they would be the start of a small herd. Next spring she would sell the wool in town.

Luke liked the lambs. They butted him playfully as he fed them. The lambs were new on the farm. Mr. Carson, the nearest neighbor, had sold them to Mr. Reed just a few weeks ago. The Carsons' well had run dry. "My wife hated it here anyway," Mr. Carson told them when he delivered the lambs. "She says she will die if she can't be somewhere she can look out her window and see people and trees. I'm going to take her back to Kentucky to stay with her mother. Then I'm heading for California."

"Foolishness," Mr. Reed muttered after Mr. Carson left.

Nevertheless, the news about the Carsons' well worried him. One day they loaded the tub and all the buckets on the wagon and drove to the river. The muddy water they brought back was good enough for the trees and the garden. With the extra water the garden at least was doing well. Luke helped his mother in the evenings, hoeing the weeds that might rob the vegetables of precious moisture.

"Do you hate it here like Mrs. Carson did?" he asked one evening while they worked.

His mother rested a minute on her hoe. "It does get pretty lonesome," she replied. "But there's a beauty here too. I guess I'm happy enough. Your father told me about Eli's offer. Would you like that, do you think?"

Luke nodded. "More than anything."

His mother went back to her hoeing without speaking, but for the first time Luke felt a glimmer of hope.

The days passed, and every morning Luke got up with a weak feeling in his stomach. Was this the day Uncle Eli would leave? So far he seemed content to stay, helping his brother with some of the heavier work on the farm during the day and teaching his nieces and nephews at night.

Uncle Eli had been there for a week when Luke's mother announced she was getting low on fuel for cooking. Sometimes they used prairie grass twisted together, but the buffalo droppings burned with a hot, nearly odorless flame.

Michael and Caleb groaned. They did not enjoy the job of walking about with two huge cloth bags their mother had sewn and filling them with the droppings. Luke did not really mind. It gave him a chance to be alone, away from the chatter of his brothers and sisters.

After a breakfast of griddle cakes and molasses Luke put a bridle on Jack and rode away from the farm. Uncle Eli had offered to let Luke ride Beauty. But after she nearly threw him when a chipmunk ran in front of her, Luke decided he preferred the dependable Jack.

Luke set Jack at a brisk trot. The prairie stretched into the horizon, mile after mile of level fields of grass, some as tall as a man. It was lonely, and there was always the danger of snakes. But there were also small bits of beauty: a dot of blue cornflowers, a flurry of startled quail, and even a glimpse of the tremendous herds of buffalo. Luke's father said he didn't think the buffalo would be here much longer. They were slowly being driven west into the Kansas Indian lands as more and more settlers tilled the prairie.

Luke hoped that would not happen. He loved

the magnificent beasts. He had tried to draw one once, a bull nearly as tall as a man, his beard dusty, his hide scarred. Luke had seen him as they drove the wagon to Georgetown. The animal was standing apart from the herd. Perhaps he was old and ready to die, or perhaps he had been driven off by one of the younger, stronger bulls. In the distance Luke had seen the herd, thousands and thousands of buffalo. "What if people settle the Indian lands someday?" Luke had asked.

Mr. Reed had shrugged. "The buffalo will still be here. The Indians have hunted them for years, and there are still millions of them. Anyway, there will never be enough settlers to drive them out."

The buffalo were the reason his father made sure the fences were always in good order. He worried that the great herd would trample down the fields of corn.

After riding for several miles, Luke found what he was looking for. There was no sign of the herd, but it had been through this area long enough ago that the sun had dried the droppings into flat, round shapes. A small stream, nearly dry now but with enough wetness left to grow a few trees along its banks, meandered across the prairie on its way to the river. Luke tied Jack to one of the trees and went on foot to fill his sacks. So many buffalo had passed through that he was able to finish his task in a very few minutes.

Luke was pleased with himself. No one at home would expect him back so soon. He trudged slowly along the dusty trail, looking for his favorite spot. The prairie sun burned high in the sky. It was hot, more so than the day before, and the grass was brown and dry. The hint of a storm they'd noticed that morning had been baked away.

At one side of the trail there was a large flat rock surrounded by several boulders. Luke had never shown this spot to anyone. It was his own secret place. He always marveled at the level rock, wondering if it had once been part of a mountain. Perhaps time and weather had worn it down until it was nearly as flat as the rest of the prairie. He poked around the boulders with a stick, making sure there were no snakes.

He sat on a boulder to catch his breath, shook the dust from his wide-brimmed hat and reached inside his shirt. His new crayons were there inside a small leather pouch.

Using the rock as a table, Luke pulled out paper and sketched quickly. The prairie was easy. He'd drawn it many times. This time, however, he almost managed to capture the *real* prairie, the sweeping greens and golds of the earth and the endless blue of the sky. Near a small rock was an Indian paintbrush flower. He drew it in the corner of his painting, a gay little flag of red. With a pleased smile, he looked at the picture. It was the best he'd ever done. He could almost imagine his mother there in a pose he'd seen often, holding to her hat against the prairie wind. With sudden inspiration he drew her there, the dusty blue of her dress blending into the sky.

With a start he realized how much time had gone by. He looked at the sun, dropping low in the sky. He'd missed the afternoon milking. His father was going to be furious. Luke rolled up the picture reluctantly and shouldered the bags of buffalo chips.

Jack was waiting where he had left him. He

threw the bags over the old horse's broad back and, grabbing a handful of mane, hauled himself up.

"Come on, Jack," he urged. Jack set off at a gallop. The horse could always be counted on to find his way back to the barn.

In a few minutes Luke saw the house and the neatly fenced fields of corn and flax. Off to the east the sky was dark. He could see jagged bursts of lightning, followed by the rumble of distant thunder. The storm sounded far away, but ahead of it the clouds boiled and seemed to touch the ground.

Something about the clouds made him look again. "Fire," he yelled, even though no one could hear. Those were not storm clouds at all. What he was seeing was a grass fire, a sweeping wall of flames. It was a good distance away but moving fast. And it was headed right for the farm.

SEVEN

Fire!

A sob caught in Luke's throat as he and Jack pounded down the dusty trail toward the sod house. Where was everyone? Could it be that they were all inside at supper, unaware of the danger sweeping across the prairie?

"Fire!" he screamed again.

His father came out of the barn door. Luke's heart sank. He was doing the milking. But there was no time to think of that now. He pointed with his arm at the horizon.

Mr. Reed raced for the house, but the rest of the

61

family were already pouring out the door. Luke reined Jack to a stop and tied him securely to a rail.

His father threw him a bucket. "Fill it!" Mr. Reed yelled as he ran for another.

Luke worked furiously, filling up bucket after bucket. Mr. Reed threw the water over the sod house. Uncle Eli helped Luke pull up the precious water. The fire was moving faster than anyone could have believed. Sharp-smelling smoke filled the air, burning Luke's throat and nose and filling his eyes with tears.

"Should we try to make it to the river?" Mrs. Reed screamed, tugging at her husband.

The river was nearly two miles away. Luke saw the fear in his father's eyes. If the fire spread between his family and the river, they would be trapped. "We'll never make it," his father said. "We'll have to face it here."

Earlier that spring Mr. Reed had carefully cleared a circle all around the house and barn as a firebreak. Uncle Eli took over filling the buckets, and they passed them down a line from Luke to Mrs. Reed and finally to Luke's father, who wet

down the circle. By now the smoke was so thick they could hardly see. As a safety measure they wet down one another.

"Take the children down in the fruit cellar," Mr. Reed yelled.

Mrs. Reed ran into the house and grabbed up the baby. She handed her to Michael while she swung open the fruit cellar doors.

"I want to help fight the fire," Michael cried.

Mrs. Reed screamed over the noise of the fire. "No! You and Caleb take care of your sisters and the baby."

Reluctantly the younger children entered the fruit cellar. Mrs. Reed closed the doors and wet them down with another bucketful of water.

The fire rolled across the prairie grass, consuming everything in its path. They could hear it now, an angry roar of destruction. Sparks flew through the air, stinging their faces and arms.

Luke's parents and Uncle Eli wet down cloth feed sacks to fight the flames. Jack reared in panic, bubbles of sweat rolling off his shoulders. Luke threw some water on him too.

Ahead of the flames, Luke saw hundreds of small

shapes—pronghorn antelope, rabbits, mice, foxes, prairie chickens, even snakes—heading for the river, in a race for their lives.

The fire skipped over the fields of corn and reached the edge of the circle. Now would come the test. If they could keep the fire from jumping the circle, they would survive. Luke felt the searing heat, and his lungs burned. It was hard to hear over the roar of the flames.

"Keep filling the buckets," Mr. Reed shouted.

Luke filled bucket after bucket. His arms ached, and his hands were blistered from the rope. Uncle Eli and Luke's parents beat at the edge of the circle with the wet cloth sacks. Suddenly Uncle Eli cheered. With no new fuel the flames seemed to shrink. The wall of fire died back to a few red-hot coals and then to black soot. As quickly as it had begun, it was gone.

Mrs. Reed shrieked. A singed place at the bottom of her long skirt had suddenly burst into flame. Mr. Reed saw it first. He raced over, knocked her down to the ground, and rolled her over and over on the wet sacks.

"Are you burned?" Luke asked anxiously.

Mrs. Reed's skirt was charred black, but her long petticoat, though scorched, had protected her legs. Miraculously the only burns were two small ones on her hands. Mr. Reed gave a victorious shout and grabbed them in a hug. "We beat it," he yelled happily. The doors to the fruit cellar swung open slowly, and Caleb peeked out.

"It's all right," said Mr. Reed. "It's out."

The younger children climbed out of the cellar. The twins' eyes were red and swollen from crying. Luke thought of how frightened they must have been, hiding down in the dark. He grabbed their hands and twirled them in a wild celebration dance. "We were afraid," announced Mary Alice and Catherine Louise.

His face was streaked with soot, and tiny burns stung there and on his hands, but Luke was so happy just to be alive that he hardly noticed.

But the celebration was short-lived. Suddenly Mrs. Reed moaned. Wordlessly she pointed to the barn. A stray spark had ignited the straw roof, and now it blazed into flame. Luke thought of the livestock—the cows still waiting in the barn for the milking, and the baby lambs. And Beauty! Luke bolted toward the barn before his mother could stop him. He heard Uncle Eli pounding behind him. Uncle Eli picked up a lamb and handed it out the door to Luke. Caleb and Michael had followed them and were busy shooing the chickens close to the house. Luke saw that his father had a rope around Maud and was leading her out.

Uncle Eli grabbed Beauty and was hurrying her to the door when she suddenly broke loose and ran back into the deepest corner of the barn. Mrs. Reed came running with a wet feed sack. "Throw it over her eyes," she screamed. Nodding, Uncle Eli rushed back into the barn and disappeared into the smoky darkness. Luke bit his lip nervously, waiting for him to reemerge. Beauty trembled with fear, but with her eyes covered she remained docile enough for Uncle Eli to lead her away from the collapsing building. Donovan nervously followed.

Luke counted the animals to make sure they were all safe.

His father had already propped a ladder against the barn. There was no time to rest. Once again they formed a bucket line. This time Caleb and Michael helped too. Uncle Eli was next to the ladder. He passed the buckets up to his brother, who threw the water on the flames. At last that fire also flickered and died. Although the roof had a large hole, the barn was saved.

Just as his father climbed back down the ladder, a drop of rain fell on Luke's head. "Look at that," Mr. Reed said. Droplets fell faster and faster. Luke's father bowed his head, and suddenly his shoulders shook as though he were racked with sobs. He put his arms around his wife, and they knelt, clinging to each other, while all around the cooling rain soaked into the parched earth.

One by one the children gathered around their parents until they all knelt, arms entwined, Uncle Eli too, looking at the ruins of their farm.

Mr. Reed raised his head, and Luke realized he was not crying at all. He was laughing. It was pouring now, and the rain turned the soot into black, sticky rivers of gunk. Mr. Reed shook his fist at the prairie and the unseen forces of nature. "You've done your worst," he said with a bitter laugh, "but I will win in the end. Just you wait and see."

EIGHT

Uncle Eli's Idea

The fire had destroyed all the newly planted corn, and the prairie was littered with the carcasses of animals that had not been able to escape its fury. Still, everyone knew it could have been much worse. None of the Reeds was hurt, and the house and animals were saved. What's more, the fire had cleared some of the land.

Mr. Reed walked across the field and kicked at the black ash that had once been tightly matted prairie grass. "Some good might come of this fire," he said. "I believe if I plow this now, it might be all right for planting next year."

It was late at night and the children were in bed. Luke, however, was not asleep. He heard Uncle Eli say in a low voice, "What will you do now?"

His father's voice came clearly from the other side of the canvas wall. "I don't know. It's too late to get in a crop. We still have the vegetable garden. If I plow all fall, then maybe next spring I could plant a full eighty acres of corn. But I won't have enough money for seed. Maybe Mr. Kline will wait for his money. Or maybe I can get a job in town this winter." Mr. Reed sounded tired and sad. "If I sell all the animals, there would be enough to rent a house."

"I will lend you the money," said Uncle Eli. Then he said, "Don't shake your head at me. You're my brother. Why would you take credit from the scoundrel Kline? You can pay me back just as easy as him."

There was a pause, and Luke could imagine his father shaking his head with his familiar stubborn look.

"I will think on it," Mr. Reed said stiffly. "I thank you for the offer."

"I've been thinking," said Mrs. Reed. "Without the crops you will not have as much need for Luke's help. Perhaps we should reconsider letting him go with Eli, at least until next spring."

Luke had almost drifted off to sleep. Hearing that, he sat straight up in bed, breathlessly waiting for his father's reply.

"He's a bright lad," Uncle Eli added. "He has a thirst for knowledge. And I think he has real talent as an artist. With me he can take in some of the country, and I will see to his studies."

"He's too young," answered Mr. Reed.

"He's older than you and I were when we were apprenticed. And he would be with family. I love him almost as much as you do."

"You spent all those years at the mill that you hated," said Mrs. Reed to her husband. "Is that what you want for your son? A talent like his is a gift from the Lord. How can you see what he can do with his paints and not know that?"

"And perhaps he will not be a great artist,"

Uncle Eli said. "Perhaps he will learn business or even come back to the farm. At least, with an education, he can choose."

"I see I am outnumbered," said Mr. Reed. "Does he want to go, do you know?"

Luke wanted to burst through the canvas and shout *yes,* but now he wasn't so sure. Uncle Eli had told him of Boston with its fine brick homes and cobblestoned streets. He thought of the luxury of sketching anytime he wanted. And of attending school. Before Uncle Eli came, that would not have sounded like a good idea. Now he couldn't wait. Uncle Eli had told him there were even books that taught you how to draw. But to leave his family— suddenly that did not seem so wonderful. Tired and confused, he stretched out on the bed.

Luke was sure he could never go to sleep, but the next thing he knew the sun was shining. His father was drinking a cup of coffee when he stumbled out for breakfast.

"I suppose you heard last night?" Mr. Reed asked.

"Yes, sir," Luke admitted, embarrassed to confess

he had been eavesdropping on the adults' conversation.

Mr. Reed did not seem to mind that he had been listening. "I do not understand this love you have for making pictures. But perhaps I have been wrong to expect my dream to be yours. Your mother and Eli seem to think this would be a good thing for you. It's a long journey, and you are very young to leave home. But if you want to go, I'll give you my blessing."

Luke threw his arms around his father. Mr. Reed patted his head. "Are you sure you won't be homesick? I can't promise how long it will be before you see us again."

Luke looked at his brothers and sisters. Michael and Caleb were throwing the cornstalk dolls to each other over their sisters' heads while the twins unhappily tried to get them back. Mary Alice kicked Michael on the shin.

"That's not very ladylike," Michael said, teasing with his mother's voice.

Mary Alice kicked him again. Harder this time. "Oh," Michael cried, dropping the dolls. The twins grabbed them and ran away, their bare feet pounding in the black soot that covered everything.

Mrs. Reed came out the door. "Caleb! Michael! Are you teasing your sisters again?"

Luke laughed, seeing the boys' innocent looks. "No, Mama," Caleb said quickly. "I don't know what got into those girls. Maybe the fire made 'em go crazy or something. They just came by and started kicking and yelling. Then they ran away. And we were just on our way to do some chores too."

Mrs. Reed nodded. "I'm glad to hear you say that. I could use some help washing this soot off the walls."

As Caleb and Michael headed into the house with crestfallen faces, a smile twitched on Mr. Reed's lips, but Luke suddenly felt a pang of sadness. How he would miss them!

He straightened his shoulders. "I want to go."

"Then I will tell Eli," Mr. Reed said.

Now that the decision was made, life seemed to move at lightning speed. A dozen times the next day Luke fought off the urge to change his mind. Mrs. Reed packed a small canvas bag with

Luke's clothing. He carefully placed his crayons on top.

Early the next morning Uncle Eli saddled Beauty. Luke would ride Donovan, the packhorse.

The family came outside to say their good-byes. The twins were crying. "We don't want you to go," they sobbed together.

Luke felt like crying himself. "Don't cry," he said. "I know what. I'll draw pictures of everything I see and send them to you."

"Make us proud of you," Mr. Reed said. "Remember all that we have taught you."

"I will," Luke promised.

His mother squeezed him hard. There were tears in her eyes, but she smiled. "Eli has promised to bring you home next spring, sooner if you are too homesick."

Caleb and Michael gravely shook his hand, and then Luke mounted Donovan. With a final wave they were off. Luke twisted in the saddle, waving until the sod house and his family were no more than tiny dots upon the horizon. Uncle Eli smiled, but already Luke felt a wave of homesickness wash over him. When would he see the Iowa farm again?

NINE

---◆---

The Journey
to Independence

The first day the road led them through several small towns, much like Georgetown. In between each was the prairie. Where the fire had not spread, the grass was taller than Uncle Eli. It grew on either side of the road, making it seem as though they were the only people in the world. Uncle Eli sang to make the time pass by, and he taught the words to Luke.

"Jimmy crack corn and I don't care,
Jimmy crack corn and I don't care."

"What does that song mean?" Luke asked.

Uncle Eli smiled. "Danged if I know. Catchy tune, though, don't you think?"

Luke agreed. He wiggled uncomfortably in the pack saddle. His legs were cramped, and his behind was getting sore.

In the late afternoon a large rabbit jumped out of the grass, and Uncle Eli shot him. There was a faint line of trees ahead, marking a stream. "Looks like a good place to set up for the night," Uncle Eli said.

Luke jumped off Donovan and promptly fell on his face. His legs were numb. He finally stood up, but his legs felt bowed, as if he were still on his horse.

Uncle Eli looked sympathetic. "You'll get used to it in a few days."

"I hope so," Luke said ruefully. "I'm mighty sore."

"I've got some salve for that," Uncle Eli said, pulling a jar from one of the bags packed on Donovan.

It seemed that Uncle Eli was ready for just about anything. They gathered some dried driftwood to make a fire. He took a bit of flint from his tinder-box, struck his knife against it, and was rewarded with a tiny spark. He added tiny twigs and then larger branches until a good fire blazed. Luke un-saddled the horses and took them to the river to drink while his uncle skinned and cleaned the rabbit. From somewhere Uncle Eli pulled out a frying pan. Using forked branches, he balanced the pan a few inches above the fire. Then he put in a lump of lard and rolled the rabbit pieces in flour. "Wait till you taste this," he said cheerfully.

Luke's stomach was making strange noises, but he wasn't sure he could stay awake long enough to eat. His eyelids dropped shut.

"This will keep you awake," Uncle Eli said, handing him a tin cup filled with hot strong coffee.

The coffee gave him enough energy to stay awake until the rabbit was cooked. Uncle Eli was right. It was delicious.

They were on the road again by dawn. Luke was so sore that he wasn't sure he could stand another day. Only the thought of pleasing his uncle kept him going. By the end of the day he was sure nothing could be more painful, but he was wrong. The next day was even worse.

As his uncle lay snoring softly beside him, Luke stared at the stars. He would beg Uncle Eli to let him return home. This was a horrible mistake. Right now he should be asleep next to his brothers. His mother would tuck in the cover and brush a kiss on his forehead with a soft good-night. Tears of self-pity fell out of the corners of his eyes and across his cheeks. It was a long time before he fell asleep.

The next morning a strange thing happened that made him change his mind. He actually felt better. When he stood up, he realized that his muscles no longer ached and that the homesickness of the night had passed. He managed a cheerful whistle while he made the morning coffee.

"The worst is over," Uncle Eli said, giving him a wink. "You are a man of the road now."

Luke didn't admit how close he had been to giving up, but he suspected Uncle Eli knew. They ate quickly and were soon on their way. Luke took a little more interest in his surroundings. The land had changed while he'd been so busy suffering. It was less flat, and greener, and there were more trees. They were seeing more travelers too. Several time they passed wagons, and they caught a glimpse of a large wagon with a canvas cover following a short distance behind them.

"It's called a Conestoga wagon," Uncle Eli explained. "Probably someone wanting to join up with a wagon train for Oregon. Folks say there's mighty good land there."

About noon they came to a broad, muddy river. "The Missouri," Uncle Eli told Luke. "We'll have to ferry across."

They found the ferry at the end of the road. There were other people waiting to cross, and Luke looked at them curiously while Uncle Eli gave the man two silver dollars for their fare.

"Never thought much about there being so many people in the world before," Luke said when his uncle returned.

Uncle Eli smiled as they led the horses onto the long flat barge. "You haven't seen anything yet," he said. "Independence is just about the liveliest place you'll ever see. Just about anyone going to Oregon or California starts off there."

But even Uncle Eli was amazed when they got to the city. The streets were a mass of noise and confusion. The big covered wagons rumbled across the roads, adding to the braying of mules and the throngs of people all hurrying about their unknown business. Men shouted orders as freight from the East was unloaded into the merchants' stores. Others haggled over the prices of barrels of flour, cornmeal, molasses, and beans. There were street vendors hawking axes, picks, and guidebooks to the California goldfields. It seemed to Luke that about every other shop was a wheelwright's or a blacksmith's. People were lined up trying to get wheels fixed and buy chains, linchpins, and axles. Everywhere he looked, there was something new to see.

They finally found a small inn, on a side street somewhat removed from the confusion. Beauty and Donovan were tethered outside. There was a small restaurant at street level and a sign advertising rooms for rent upstairs. The dining room was

pleasantly decorated with white curtains and flow-
ered wallpaper. It was midafternoon, too early for
most people to want dinner. There were only two
other customers, quietly eating at a corner table.
Uncle Eli chose a table away from them and
ordered dinner from a tired-looking woman with
a stained apron. She returned from the kitchen in
a few minutes with steaming platefuls of chicken
stew and biscuits. Luke picked up his spoon and
shoveled his food into his mouth. It wasn't as good
as his mother's, but it was the first decent meal
they'd had since Uncle Eli had killed the rabbit
days earlier. "I never ate in a restaurant before,"
he volunteered.

"Slow down. Taste it before you swallow," Uncle
Eli advised him. He ate his own food slowly with
his fork and wiped his mouth between bites.

Embarrassed, Luke picked up his fork. "We don't
have these at home," he said. He tried to scoop up
some gravy, but it fell between the tines. "My
stars!" he exclaimed, borrowing his mother's
expression. "How do you eat wet food with this
thing?"

"You use the spoon for that," Uncle Eli said with a chuckle.

"Seems pretty foolish to me, all that trading back and forth. A spoon will catch just about anything."

Uncle Eli laughed out loud. "You may be right." He waited until Luke had finished eating and said, "I have some business to attend to. Can you find your way back here if I allow you to look around?"

After Luke had promised not to get lost, his uncle hurried off on his business. Before he left, he gave Luke a few coins. "Buy yourself some candy," he said.

Luke wandered down the street. He bought some cinnamon sticks at a bustling general store. Farther down the street was a blacksmith's shop. Luke stopped for a while to watch the red-faced blacksmith hammer a wheel into shape, then walked on, sucking the sugary candy and looking in the shop windows.

When he reached the end of the street, Luke crossed to the other side. "Look out, boy," someone shouted. Luke jumped on the sidewalk, narrowly missing being run over by a large wagon pulled by eight strong oxen. Once his heart stopped pounding, Luke collected himself and spent an hour exploring as much of the city as he wanted to see. Before he returned to the inn, he checked out a nearby livery stable. The horses seemed content, and the owner was a pleasant fellow who promised to take good care of their horses.

Uncle Eli had still not returned, so Luke settled on the wide porch that ran across the front of the inn. He pulled out a clean sheet of paper and a pencil and started to sketch the busy street. Suddenly he was struck with a longing for home. He started another picture, this time using the precious crayons from the tin. He drew the prairie, the tall grass bending to the wind and a dark storm boiling in the sky.

"I never saw anyone draw like that," said the waitress. Luke had not heard her come out on the porch. "I have a room at the back of the inn. That picture would look pretty nice on my wall. I could give you twenty-five-cents."

Gleefully Luke put the finishing touches on his sketch. He had to fight the urge to jump up and holler with pride. She wanted to pay real money for one of his pictures. The waitress sat down and kicked off her shoes while she waited. Luke could see them out of the corner of his eye. They were made out of a piece of leather sewn Indian style. There was a hole in the toe of one, and he noticed that the bottom of her dress had been patched.

"This is just a sort of practice picture," he said. "Wouldn't be fair to charge someone. I'll give it to you, though."

The woman snatched up the picture as though she was afraid he might change his mind. "I'll take good care of it," she promised.

They sat in silence for a minute, and then Luke said politely, "That was mighty good eating we had today."

The waitress smiled. "I don't do the cooking. I just serve it."

"Oh," Luke said. "Well, you served it pretty well."

The woman laughed. "Well, thank you. Don't get many compliments around here. You and your daddy going west?"

"That's my uncle," Luke explained. "My daddy's back in Iowa. Uncle Eli is taking me to Boston."

"You're about the only one going east, I'll wager. Everyone else is heading for California. I'm considering it myself."

"Do you think there is really any gold there?" Luke asked.

The woman shook her head. "Don't know. But at this rate half the men in the country will be there. I figure maybe some of them will be looking for wives soon enough. Maybe I can find me one of those men with some of that gold."

Luke didn't know what to say to that. "Good luck," he said after a minute.

"You too," she said, and got up to go back inside the inn. "Thanks again for the picture."

A wagon rumbled by after she'd gone inside. "California or Bust!" was written on the canvas cover. Luke shook his head. People sure were peculiar. He took out his tablet again and quickly started sketching.

TEN

On to St. Louis

Uncle Eli returned, looking pleased with himself. "You know, your father wouldn't let me lend him money."

"He's proud," Luke said.

Uncle Eli nodded. "And stubborn. But he'll have to take this. I just arranged for a house to be delivered."

"A house?" Luke gasped.

"Well, he'll have to build it. But there's lumber and nails and shingles for the roof. There are also a couple of window panes. Even Jeremiah is not stubborn enough to let all that good lumber go to waste."

Luke grinned, thinking of his mother's face when she saw the lumber. "Mama will make sure it's not wasted," he said.

"I tried to find my partners. Guess they got tired of waiting and headed back east. We might catch up to them later," Uncle Eli said. "Maybe in Saint Louis. Right now all I want is a hot bath and a good night's sleep. Let's see if we can find a livery stable to bed down these horses."

"I found a nice one just down the street," Luke said. "The horses there seemed well cared for."

"Good boy," Uncle Eli said.

They took the horses to the stable, and Uncle Eli paid the man a dollar for each and another dollar to watch the saddles and bridles.

The next morning the waitress winked when she saw Luke. "That's a mighty fine nephew you have there," she told Uncle Eli as she gave Luke an extra hunk of butter for his hotcakes.

"I think so too," Uncle Eli said.

Luke blushed. It was embarrassing to have them talk about him that way as though he wasn't even there. He ate slowly with his fork, laying it across his plate as Uncle Eli did when he was done. "You're a fast learner," his uncle said.

"Luke tells me that you are going east," the waitress said. "Beware. I've heard they have the cholera in Saint Louis. Only yesterday a family came through who'd buried two babies a week ago, poor things. The husband told me they were well in the morning and by nightfall they were dead. The wife looked none too well to me. But perhaps that was only the grief that made her look so pale."

Luke had heard of cholera, a disease that moved with deadly swiftness.

"Thank you for the warning," Uncle Eli said seriously. "We'll stay only long enough to cross the river."

After breakfast they picked up the horses and rode out of town. Independence was an interesting place, Luke thought, but he wasn't sorry to be leaving the noise and confusion.

"Is Boston like Independence?" he asked, the third day after they'd left the city.

Uncle Eli shook his head no. "It's bigger, but a

lot quieter. And of course you'll see the ocean. More water than you've ever seen."

"That Missouri River was more water than I'd ever seen," Luke admitted.

"At Saint Louis we'll cross the mighty Mississippi. It's much bigger than the Missouri. But both of them put together wouldn't make a drop in the ocean."

Luke tried to picture all that water. "That must be something," he said.

Uncle Eli smiled. "You'd better save your blue crayon."

There were plenty of small towns and inns along the way, so Luke felt well fed and rested. It seemed, however, that they were the only ones heading east. Time after time they had to move over to let one of the giant covered wagons pass by. Luke watched them with a thoughtful expression.

"I've been thinking," Luke said. "Even if there was gold out west in California, would it be enough for all these people?"

"I suppose some of these fools will just stay

there anyway," Uncle Eli said. "I hear it's good farming land. And they don't have any winters."

To Luke, used to the fierce ones in Iowa, that sounded like a wondrous thing.

"Do you suppose they will build towns in California?" Luke asked. "Seems like they will have to be building some towns and stores like back there in Independence."

Uncle Eli laughed. "I knew you were a smart one. I've been thinking that same thing myself. Maybe you and I should take a load of supplies to California."

Luke shook his head. Things were never dull around Uncle Eli. He hadn't even managed to get to Boston and his uncle was talking about turning right around.

A sudden summer storm had been brewing while they talked. Black clouds boiled overhead, and distant booms of thunder shook the skies. Ahead another wagon rolled toward them. The driver seemed to be having trouble controlling his team of oxen.

"City folk," Uncle Eli snorted.

Suddenly a bolt of lightning cracked close by. Beauty pranced nervously, and Uncle Eli patted her, trying to keep her calm.

"Look out," he yelled. The driver had been so startled by the thunder that he had dropped the reins. Unrestrained, the team had bolted, gathering speed while the wagon rocked from side to side. The man clung to the seat, and as the wagon rumbled past, Luke saw that his face was white with terror. Several frightened children looked out from under the canvas cover. Luke jerked the reins, turning Donovan.

The sight of the children spurred Uncle Eli into action too. He kicked in his heels, and Beauty galloped after the runaway team. Before Luke could catch up to the wagon, Uncle Eli had overtaken the lead oxen and, reaching down, managed to grab the yoke. "Whoa!" he yelled until the oxen finally stopped. They pawed the ground, panting, but Uncle Eli talked calmly to them until they settled down. The driver climbed down and picked up the reins. He said something to Uncle Eli, but Luke's uncle merely waved and trotted back to Luke.

"You saved that man's life!" Luke exclaimed.

Uncle Eli seemed distracted. He was frowning as he dismounted and ran his hands down Beauty's leg.

"What's wrong?" Luke asked.

Uncle Eli took the reins and led his horse slowly up the road. "I'm not sure. She may have hurt her leg running after that wagon. Let's camp here," Uncle Eli said, pointing to a small stream near the road.

Thunder rumbled again, farther away this time. "We'd better hurry and make camp," said Uncle Eli as he tore strips from a shirt to make a bandage for Beauty. Her foreleg was definitely swollen, and she was starting to limp. While Uncle Eli worked with her, Luke took a bamboo pole and fished the stream. He was quickly rewarded. He caught four fish. They were small, but big enough for a meal.

It had seemed as though the storm would miss them, but just as they finished eating a heavy rain started, and in only a few minutes they were soaked. Luke had been enjoying the prospect of sleeping outside again, but now he groaned, thinking of the damp, muddy night ahead. A man was approaching in the darkening gloom. "I'm Edward Gates," he said. "This here is my land you're camping on."

Uncle Eli started to apologize, but Mr. Gates waved his hand. "Don't matter, long as you're gone tomorrow. Ordinarily my wife would have insisted you come to the house for dinner. But with all this cholera around we're inclined to be more careful. Got six daughters, and one of them is kind of frail."

Mr. Gates took a breath as though he wasn't used to such long speeches. "Anyway, you are welcome to stay in the barn," he continued, pointing across the pasture, "Be a lot drier in the hay." He handed something to Uncle Eli. "Peach cobbler," he said. "My wife sent it for you and the boy."

They thanked Mr. Gates and led the horses to the barn. The peach cobbler turned out to be even better than it looked. Luke went to bed comfortable, full, and warm.

The next morning Beauty's leg was still swollen. They walked the remaining miles, but even so, by the time they approached Saint Louis, the horse was limping badly.

Rain still pelted them, drenching their clothes and their spirits.

"I had hoped we would not stay any time in Saint Louis, what with the cholera and all, but I think we must," Uncle Eli said as they walked through the outskirts of the city.

Saint Louis was even bigger than and almost as noisy as Independence. Nervously Luke looked for signs of cholera. He was surprised to see so many people bustling about on business. Uncle Eli took a room in the first inn they came to. It was old and run-down. The sign was so weather-worn that Uncle Eli could hardly read it, and the once-white fence was gray. There was a small stable in back, however, and the innkeeper seemed friendly.

Leaving Luke alone in their room, Uncle Eli went to tend Beauty. When he returned, he looked grim. "She'll be all right with some rest. But there is no way she'll be ready to travel for a couple of weeks."

"What will we do?" Luke asked.

"The innkeeper thinks he knows someone who might give me a fair price for the horses," Uncle

Eli said. "If he does, we'll take a barge to the other side of the river in the morning. He says we might have trouble getting across. There was a terrible fire on the riverfront, and a lot of the ships burned. Barges too."

"What'll we do if we can't make it?" Luke asked.

"We'll make it," Uncle Eli assured him. "Then we'll get a stagecoach heading east for Indianapolis."

A stagecoach! Luke was having a hard time taking it all in.

Uncle Eli was unusually silent all evening. Luke knew he was grieving over losing Beauty. As for himself, he would miss Donovan too. So much had happened in the last weeks that home seemed almost like another life. He thought of his family and sighed. It was the first time in days he'd had time to think about how much he missed them.

When Luke woke up the next morning, Uncle Eli was gone. After a few minutes of panic Luke was relieved when his uncle returned, looking more cheerful.

"Sold them to a nice fellow," he said. "He's going to give the horses to his daughters. In the meantime they'll have a nice grassy pasture. Now for the Mississippi!"

They ate quickly and walked to the riverfront. Once again Luke was nearly overwhelmed by the sights. The morning fog made the air misty and cool. From a rise above the water he could see the devastation caused by the fire. On street after street hollow black shells of buildings stood empty and silent. Along the remains of a long wharf were the burned-out hulks of ship after ship.

Uncle Eli shook his head. "I'd heard there was a fire, but I never imagined this."

"How did it happen?" Luke asked.

An old man sitting on a bench had overheard them. "Was the wind," he said. "The *White Cloud* started burning. They had all that hemp for making rope piled on the dock, and the next thing you know the fire was spreading. Spread to the ships too. More than twenty of them burned up."

Uncle Eli pointed to workmen busy near the waterfront. "Looks like they've already started to rebuild."

The old man nodded proudly. "Started just a couple of days after the fire. You come back next year, I imagine you won't know there ever was such a thing."

A steamboat was loading passengers. Luke peeked in as they passed. A crystal chandelier sparkled in the morning light in a room filled with brocaded couches and chairs. Well-dressed men and women strolled toward the dock on their way to board. The ladies daintily held up their skirts when they crossed the charred boards of the dock.

Uncle Eli had something a little less fancy in mind. He bought passage on a barge loaded with barrels and boxes of goods that was about to cross the river. The crossing was smooth and easy, and as soon as they docked, they hurried to the stagecoach office.

"You're in luck," the man said as he sold them the tickets. "Stage leaves in just a few minutes."

Outside the ticket office several men were hitching a fresh team of horses. The coach was a bright burgundy with gold designs painted on the door. The inside was lined with a silky cloth. There were two long seats that faced each other and a padded bench in the middle for extra passengers. The top of the coach was flat, and two scruffy-looking men threw Luke's bag on top with the other luggage.

Luke looked curiously at his fellow passengers as they boarded. There were two well-dressed men with leather traveling cases and an old lady saying good-bye to a family with a lot of kids. Somebody's grandmother, Luke supposed, going home after a visit. At the last minute a man and woman came running up with several bags and boxes. The drivers grumbled, but they hefted their baggage to the top, then had tied everything down.

Uncle Eli sat with the traveling men. The old woman settled beside the man and his wife on the opposite seat. Luke had to sit on the middle seat, which was no more than a backless bench.

At least he had the whole bench to himself. If he got tired, he could stretch out. He sat down facing his uncle. He was barely settled when the drivers climbed up to their seat. There was a crack of a whip, and the coach jerked forward. Luke almost fell off the bench, but Uncle Eli steadied him until he could balance himself. Luke stared out of the window and watched as, mile after mile, the stagecoach carried him to his new life.

ELEVEN

———•———

Stagecoach Adventures

The adults talked together. Luke stayed quiet and mostly listened. The two men were named Mr. Sills and Mr. Luckett. They worked for the railroad. "We've been buying land for the new railroad coming this way," explained Mr. Sills.

"You ever seen a railroad train, boy?" Mr. Luckett asked Luke.

"No, sir, I never did," Luke answered. He didn't want to admit that he didn't even know what a railroad train was, but Mr. Sills understood.

"It's the latest way of traveling," he said. "Soon there will be railroads clear across the country."

The older woman introduced herself as Mrs. Post. "I've been visiting my grandchildren for the last month," she told them. Luke smiled to himself that he had guessed correctly. Mrs. Post settled quietly in the corner and opened a book. The man and woman were newly married. Their name was Jones, and they were going all the way to Cincinnati, where the husband would be a lawyer.

There was talk of cholera and the rebuilding of the riverfront. Mrs. Post raised her head and said that no disease would keep her away from her daughter's family. The coach jolted and swayed on the rutted road. Once it hit a bump so hard that the passengers bounced up in their seats and hit their heads on the roof. This time Luke did tumble off the bench. Mrs. Post gave up trying to read and just looked out the window. There wasn't much to see. Endless miles rolled by with land very much like that which Luke had left at home, although there were more trees and more ups and downs.

After several hours there was a quick stop for

fresh horses in a small town. The passengers had only enough time for a cup of tea and a quick stretch of cramped legs before they were off again.

The next section of road was even rougher, and deep ruts made the coach sway so far to one side that Mrs. Post began to moan, "We are going to tip over. We are going to tip over."

Finally Mr. Luckett said in an impatient voice, "I assure you, dear lady, that you are perfectly safe."

Uncle Eli looked out the window. "I don't know. We do seem to be going a bit fast for the condition of the road."

The words were no sooner out of his mouth than the coach swayed again, even more violently. Mrs. Jones screamed as the coach seemed to hang suspended for a second. Then with a crash it fell over. Luke was thrown from the bench. Instantly he was smothered in a pile of legs, arms, and bodies that had fallen on top of him. The coach was still moving. It was dragged along on its side for several yards before the frightened horses finally stopped.

"Is everyone all right?" asked Uncle Eli.

"I knew we'd tip over. I knew it," exclaimed Mrs. Post. Now that it had actually happened, she seemed fairly calm.

They managed to extract themselves from the coach and checked themselves for bumps and scrapes. Luke rubbed his elbow. It was badly bruised, and there was a knot on his head. One of the drivers was on the ground, nursing a sprained leg he'd gotten when he'd jumped off the falling coach. The baggage from the top of the coach was scattered everywhere.

The second driver was unhurt. He surveyed the damage. "I think it will be all right. We just have to get her back up."

Everyone lined up on one side of the coach and slowly lifted. At last it rocked into place. The door was slightly dented, and the burgundy paint scraped, but other than that the coach seemed none the worse for wear.

The luggage was tied to the top, and they were off, this time a bit more slowly.

The passengers were hot and tired after their adventure. Luke stared out the window. An occasional line of trees marked a stream or river. A few small wood houses came into view and then were gone, and sometimes there was a larger house of brick with prosperous fields of tall corn. Luke wondered about the people in those houses. Were they families like his own?

When at last they stopped for the night, it was dark. The weary passengers climbed out of the coach, rubbing sore muscles. They were at a small stone inn. Uncle Eli told Luke the sign at the entrance said it was called the Gray Goose.

"Welcome," called the proprietor. He was a roly-poly man not much taller than Luke. He chatted with the travelers while his sour-faced wife served them dinner. In spite of her grumpy manner, the meal of boiled pork and potatoes was excellent. For dessert there was apple pie with cream.

After dinner the innkeeper lit a small lantern and led them upstairs. There was a small room for the ladies and another for the men. "Stage leaves at six in the morning," the innkeeper told them. Luke was too tired to do anything other than fall on his cot and sleep. It seemed he had scarcely closed his eyes before Uncle Eli was shaking him awake. He was given a biscuit and a cup of tea by the innkeeper's wife. Her mood had not improved.

She hurried back and forth, serving them silently, while her husband chatted with the railroad men. Stepping outside, Luke saw that they were in a town with whitewashed houses and several business establishments. Mr. Luckett and Mr. Sills were staying on here, and there was a new passenger.

The stranger was tall and unshaved, and his manner was surly. His hair was greasy and long, and he smelled so awful that Mrs. Jones held a dainty white handkerchief to her nose. He grunted his name, Barnes, leaned his head on the side of the coach, and promptly fell asleep. The passengers, who had chatted so comfortably, now lapsed into an uneasy silence.

At midday the horses were changed, and once again the passengers were given a quick meal. "Eat fast," Uncle Eli whispered while they ate.

Luke gave his uncle a questioning look but gobbled his food. Uncle Eli stretched and said in a voice loud enough to be overheard, "My legs are getting mighty cramped sitting in the coach. Think I'll walk for a bit."

"Stage leaves in ten minutes," the innkeeper said, looking at a large pocket watch.

"We'll be ready," Uncle Eli said. "Coming, Luke?"

Taking his cue from his uncle, Luke said, "I could use a walk too."

He followed his uncle outside. They walked casually to the corner of the building. Then his uncle pulled Luke quickly into an alley running behind the inn.

"Watch to see no one comes," he said, fumbling with his shirt. Luke looked around. For the moment, at least, the alley was quiet. Tied around Uncle Eli's waist was a packet he quickly untied.

"What's that?" Luke asked.

"I'm carrying a lot of money. Banknotes. It's from a good bank, not one of those wildcat operations."

Even Luke had heard of wildcat banks. They issued paper money without enough gold or silver to make the notes good.

"Pull up your shirt," Uncle Eli said tersely.

With another look around the alley, Luke obeyed. Uncle Eli quickly tied the packet around his waist. "I don't trust that Barnes fellow," Uncle Eli said. "I figure if anything happens, no one would pay any attention to a boy." He pulled Luke's shirt down and gave him an appraising look. "Good, it doesn't show at all. How does it feel?"

The packet was heavy and uncomfortable, but Luke replied, "It's fine. Do you think he means to rob us?"

Uncle Eli reached into his boot and pulled out a small pouch. "Maybe not," he answered, "but I've got a bad feeling about that fellow."

He shook out a few gold coins. "I'd look suspicious if I didn't have any money." He noticed Luke looking curiously at the coins. "Don't imagine you've ever seen one of these."

"No, sir. Pa trades for most everything we buy."

"They're called double eagles. They're worth twenty dollars." Uncle Eli put one of the coins into Luke's hand. Luke had never before held a coin worth twenty dollars. Yet here was his uncle with a whole pouch full of them.

Uncle Eli slipped the rest of the coins in his pocket. "Now put this pouch into your shoe," he said.

Suddenly Uncle Eli stiffened. Barnes was slouching down the alley right at them. His eyes squinted with suspicion.

With a burst of inspiration Luke cried out in a loud voice, "I miss my family. I want to go home." He threw himself into his uncle's arms, pretending to sob and hiding the pouch at the same time. "Just because we are poor shouldn't mean I have to be sent away."

Uncle Eli caught on immediately. He patted Luke awkwardly. He looked at Barnes and shrugged. "The boy is a bit homesick, I'm afraid."

Barnes looked disgusted. "He better not be blubbering on the stage. I don't like kids. Especially noisy ones." That said, he turned and left the alley. It was the most he had spoken all day.

Uncle Eli grinned. "Quick thinking. We'd better hurry. We don't want the stage to leave without us."

Luke slipped the pouch in his shoe and wiggled it under his toes, then walked a few steps to check. The pouch held the coins tightly enough that they did not jingle.

When the coach was ready, Barnes pushed his way in front of the others and took the seat nearest the door. The other passengers had to climb over him to get in. Ignoring the grumbling from his fellow travelers, he closed his eyes and promptly went back to sleep.

It started to rain as soon as they set off. The road became slippery with mud. Twice the wheels became stuck and the passengers had to get out and push. When Barnes stayed in the coach and refused to help, even Uncle Eli did not challenge him.

Late in the afternoon the drivers urged the horses across a wide, shallow river. It was only a few inches deep, but, just a few feet away from the opposite bank, the coach, with a sickening lurch, again tipped over onto its side. This time it fell so that Luke landed on top and Barnes was on the bottom of the heap.

Mrs. Jones shrieked, "Help, oh, help."

Barnes cursed. "Shut up, you noisy cow, and get off me."

The door lay facedown and could not be opened. Water was seeping in, soaking the tangle of people.

"Oh, my, oh, my," moaned Mrs. Post.

"I'm drowning," Barnes yelled from the bottom of the pile.

Luke managed to crawl out the open window. Uncle Eli pushed and Luke pulled, and they managed to get Mrs. Post out. Next came Uncle Eli. He pulled Mr. and Mrs. Jones out and reluctantly reached in for the fuming, angry Barnes.

"It's about time," growled Barnes as he emerged.

Uncle Eli ignored Barnes. "Is everyone all right?"

Standing on the side wall of the coach, the passengers examined themselves for injuries. Except for a few bruises, once again they had escaped unharmed, although Barnes and the Joneses were dripping wet.

"You insulted my wife," Mr. Jones sputtered.

Barnes glared at Mr. Jones. "She was right on top of me. What did you expect me to say?" In a high voice he said, "Oh, please, dear lady, do take your knee out of my eye."

"There was no need to call her a cow," Mr. Jones said, bristling.

Mr. Barnes leaned over until his face was an inch away from Mr. Jones's and said threateningly, "So what do you want to do about it?"

Uncle Eli stepped in. Patting Mr. Jones on the arm, he said, "We were all excited. I'm sure Mr. Barnes just forgot himself in the heat of the moment. We have worse things to worry about."

He pointed to the driver, who was lying in the river, unmoving. The second driver was slowly picking himself up from the riverbank, where he had been thrown.

Uncle Eli and Luke jumped down into the water. The coachman was unconscious, tangled in the reins. The reins had actually saved his life because they had kept his head out of the water. The horses neighed and pawed at the ground, dangerously close to the driver's limp body.

Mrs. Post was still wringing her hands and repeating, "Oh, my, oh, my." A murderous look from Barnes silenced her.

"Is he alive?" Barnes called down, not offering to help.

The second driver had come to his senses and

staggered into the water to help. As they lifted the still-unconscious man, a small flask tumbled from his pocket.

Uncle Eli sniffed. "He's not hurt. He's drunk."

He looked at the second driver. His eyes were dimmed and red, and he was swaying on his feet. "You're both drunk."

By now Mr. Jones had climbed down to help, but Uncle Eli dropped the driver back into the water. He fell facedown, but immediately he began to choke and sputter, then managed to pull himself into a sitting position.

"Drunk!" Mr. Jones exclaimed. "I can't believe it. We trusted our lives to these two."

"You don't know how hard it is," whined the second driver. "A little nip makes the time go by."

Uncle Eli sighed in disgust. "Let's get the coach upright and at least get out of the water."

Luke's shoes were soaked. Water squished out as he went over to the coach to help Mrs. Post. She had recovered from her shock. With a haughty sniff at Barnes she sat down and slid into the water. While she held her large skirts up with one hand, Luke helped her balance as she walked to the riverbank across the slippery stones. Mr. Jones gallantly carried his wife to shore.

Barnes pulled out a pocket watch. It looked like pure gold, and the lid was carved with leaves and vines. It was hooked to a chain that also seemed to be made of gold. The watch seemed strangely out of place in Barnes's dirty hands. Grunting in annoyance, Barnes shoved it back into his pocket and jumped down. This time he willingly took his place to help upright the coach. Luke pushed with all his might. His new shoes slipped in the mud, and he fell to his knees. After struggling to his feet again, he retook his position. "Push together," shouted Uncle Eli. "One, two, push!" Slowly the coach tipped upward, and they managed to rock it into position. Water poured out from all the cracks.

Luke ran to the bank and grabbed the harness on the lead horses. "Git up," he yelled. The horses strained to obey, but the large wheels of the coach were stuck. Groaning, the men moved to the back of the coach, and with the help of a mighty shove from them, the horses managed to pull the wagon up onto the banks.

TWELVE

Bandits!

Uncle Eli refused to let either drunken driver take the reins again. He climbed onto their seat high above the ground and motioned for Luke to sit beside him. The damp passengers climbed back inside with the two crestfallen drivers.

The adults glared at the them and grumbled. Luke was happy he did not have to ride inside the coach. He scrambled up next to his uncle.

"Ready?" Uncle Eli asked with a smile.

When Luke nodded, his uncle slapped the reins. "Git up," he shouted.

"This is fun," Luke said after a few minutes.

Uncle Eli grinned. "It is. Although I don't think I'd want to do it all the time."

"How far is it to the next town?"

"According to the driver, it's only a few more miles," Uncle Eli said cheerfully.

Suddenly Mrs. Post stuck her head out and yelled, "Mr. Reed, Mr. Reed. Stop the coach. We have an emergency and need your help."

Uncle Eli pulled on the reins until the team came to a stop. Handing the reins to Luke, he jumped down. From his high perch Luke saw his uncle open the coach door and peer in, then slowly back up.

At first Luke saw nothing wrong. The passengers climbed out one by one and slowly turned back to face the coach. Mrs. Post climbed out, looking pale. Barnes came out right behind her.

"I'm sorry, Mr. Reed," said Mrs. Post without taking her eyes off Barnes. "I had to tell you to stop the coach. He said he would shoot me if I didn't."

Then Luke saw what they were all staring at. Barnes held a revolver in his hand, and it was pointed right at Mrs. Post.

There was a clatter of hooves on the road, and a rider appeared. For a brief minute the passengers looked hopeful, thinking they were about to be rescued. Then the rider came into sight and their faces fell. The man was leading a second horse— saddled, with a bedroll tied on behind.

"You're late," growled the new comer to Barnes. If anything, he was even rougher-looking.

"Fool drivers got drunk and let the stage tip over," Barnes replied.

The second man waved a gun at Uncle Eli. "Put your hands up in the air where I can see them."

"Oh, my, oh, my," moaned Mrs. Post.

"Shut that up or I'll give you something to 'oh, my' about," Barnes said, brandishing his weapon.

Mrs. Post fell silent, but Mr. Jones sputtered, "Surely you don't mean to rob us?"

The second man laughed. "That's exactly what we mean to do. You, boy," he said, pointing to Luke. "Toss them bags down."

Luke looked at Uncle Eli, who nodded. "Do as he says."

Luke scrambled up to the flat roof. One by one he tossed the bags down on the ground. He thought about the packet tied to his waist and the pouch in his shoe. He kept his toes curled around it so the coins inside couldn't jingle.

The bandits emptied the contents of each bag along the road. The ladies blushed when their unmentionables tumbled out, but Barnes and his friend were interested in other things. They gathered several pieces of jewelry, watches, and a small purse. "What's this?" Barnes said upon opening Luke's canvas bag and seeing the small tin of crayons. Eagerly he tore it open but instantly threw it down on the road. "Crayons! I've got no need of those."

The other man looked in the ladies' purses and made Mr. Jones and Uncle Eli turn out their pockets and take off their boots. From Mr. Jones the robbers took a purseful of enough coins to make them grin happily.

"That's all the money we have," Uncle Eli said when Barnes pocketed the three coins Uncle Eli had kept when he'd given the money to Luke.

"That's your problem," Barnes said as he mounted the extra horse. With an evil grin the two men galloped away.

"We must get after them," Mr. Jones protested.

"How?" asked one of the drivers, sober now. "With a stagecoach? By the time we unharnessed the horses, they'd be miles ahead of us. We'll tell the sheriff in the next town."

The luggage was quickly repacked and returned to the top of the coach. The journey resumed with the humbled drivers again in their rightful positions.

Luke climbed inside the stage and gratefully rested his head against the back of the seat. He was beginning to think he had already lived through enough adventures to last him the rest of his life. He patted the money, tucked safely under his shirt. Uncle Eli gave him a wink. His uncle had been right. The robbers hadn't given Luke a second thought. He and his uncle still had almost all their money. He felt sorry for the others, though.

Once in town the travelers marched to the sheriff's office. "We've been after those two for a long time," the sheriff exclaimed after he had listened to a description of the bandits.

He hastily organized a posse led by a deputy, and they rode off. The posse was small, and the sheriff apologized. "Not too many able-bodied men left in town. Everyone's heading out west."

He wasn't too hopeful about the bandits' being found. "They are miles away by now," he said glumly.

The newlyweds looked stricken. "They took every bit of money we have. How will we rent a house when we reach Cincinnati?"

Mrs. Post lifted her skirts and from under a garter extracted a purse. "Let this be a lesson for you, my dears," she said sweetly, handing them some coins. "Traveling is a dangerous business."

Not to be outdone, Uncle Eli took off his boot. From a false heel he took several more coins and handed them to the Joneses. Luke stared in amazement as Uncle Eli winked at him conspiratorially.

"I'll send it back to you as soon as we are settled," Mr. Jones declared stoutly. His wife dabbed at her eyes with a handkerchief.

The stagecoach was ready to go. Two new drivers sat on board. Luke wondered about the other men. Uncle Eli did not believe they would lose their jobs. "With the whole world going west, they need those drivers," he said.

The journey settled into a dull sameness day after day. In Indianapolis they said good-bye to the Joneses. They were taking another coach south to Cincinnati. Luke was sorry to see them go. After so many days together they had become friends.

Uncle Eli invited Mrs. Post to have dinner with them, and she agreed. After a good meal of ham and vegetables and cake for dessert, Uncle Eli excused himself, explaining he had an errand. The restaurant was in a large brick hotel, and there was so much to see that Luke did not mind waiting with Mrs. Post. They were in a large room with many windows, and each table was covered with a clean white cloth. Paintings hung on the walls in ornate frames, looking very elegant. Luke wished he could get closer, to see them better, but he was afraid that would not be polite. He sat quietly watching the townspeople in their beautiful clothes, chatting with one another, while the waiters scurried to and fro with steaming platters of food.

"Is it like this in Boston?" he asked Mrs. Post.

"Oh, it is even more grand," she said. "My children want me to move nearer to them, now that my husband has passed away, but I do love Boston. I would miss the plays and concerts, and all my friends are there."

Just then Uncle Eli returned. He was carrying a package, but he did not explain his purchase until they had started out on the road once again.

After the stagecoach had gone a few miles, Uncle Eli handed the package to Luke.

"It's for me?" Luke asked. He tore open the wrapping. Inside were a tablet of paper and a pencil.

"I haven't run short of my own paper," Luke said.

"I promised your father I would see to your education," Uncle Eli reminded him. "We might as well start now." For the next hour he made Luke practice writing the alphabet.

Luke suddenly realized that the road they were traveling on was so smooth the coach hardly rocked.

"We're on the National Road," said Uncle Eli. "It's the one road that's been built by the federal government. We will have a good surface all the way to Baltimore. Someday maybe all roads will be paved like this, but for now it's the best in the country."

Mrs. Post looked up from her book. "The federal government built it, but I heard that they are turning it over to the states. The states are setting up tollhouses about every twenty miles. I heard the stage has to pay ten cents each time it comes to a tollhouse. No wonder my ticket cost nearly twenty-five dollars."

Luke stared out the window. Now that the road was so smooth, the stage was traveling fast. Uncle Eli told him they were traveling at six or seven miles an hour. "The railroads are much faster," he added. "They can go thirty miles an hour and maybe more."

Mrs. Post shook her head. "That is too fast for us humans."

"I'd like to see a railroad," Luke said. "Do you think we might?"

Uncle Eli looked thoughtful. "I'll see what I can do," he said.

The National Road was crowded with traffic, but

most of it was headed in the opposite direction. Wagon after wagon rolled by filled with families headed west, and there were freight wagons loaded with goods, pulled by long-eared mules. Suddenly the stage stopped. Across the road was a big iron gate. A burly toll collector came out of the stone tollhouse and collected ten cents before the gate was lifted.

Luke sketched quietly until it became too dark to see. He had filled up every inch of the page with the sights along the road. It was important to squeeze as much onto one page as he could, to save on the price of mailing the sketches to his family. He started to draw the bandits but changed his mind. His mother would worry, and without words there was no way to tell her how cleverly Uncle Eli had fooled them.

"The next town we come to, we will mail that to your father," Uncle Eli said. "I wish there were some way to pay for it ourselves instead of making your father pay."

"There is," Mrs. Post said. "You can buy a stamp that says the postage is already paid. I used one the last time I wrote my children. It's a wonderful idea.

I've heard they are even talking about bringing mail right to your house every day in some of the bigger cities. Wouldn't that be great?"

Now that the road was better, it was safe for the stage to travel after dark. At the next stop fresh horses were harnessed quickly and the new coachmen lit two lanterns that hung at the front of the stage. Passengers came and went, some traveling only from one stop to the next. Mrs. Post was already sleeping. Uncle Eli closed the curtains, Luke stretched out on the middle bench, and a few minutes later he was fast asleep.

THIRTEEN

———◆———

Journey's End

Their stagecoach was approaching the Ohio River, which the passengers had to cross before picking up another coach in Wheeling, West Virginia. Their journey had taken them across many rivers on the National Road, often on stone bridges that had curious S shapes. But the Ohio was different, Uncle Eli told Luke. It was a mighty river, wide and deep.

"They were building a giant suspension bridge last time I traveled west," Uncle Eli said. "It wasn't finished, but it might be by now."

The river was a busy place. A steamboat chugged by, full of passengers from the north headed to Cincinnati. Boatmen guided barges loaded with goods through the swift current.

To Luke's disappointment, however, the bridge was still not open. Once more they were forced to cross on a flatboat. Luke stared at the magnificent unfinished bridge as they slowly made their way across the deep waters of the Ohio. High above, laborers scurried about, smoothing the roadbed. "I didn't know people could build such amazing things," he said.

He sketched quickly, trying to capture every detail for his family back home.

Uncle Eli planned on resting in Wheeling for a day, but when they stopped for dinner, the inn-keeper told them there was an outbreak of cholera, and they and Mrs. Post decided to go on. Wheeling was a narrow town, caught between the river and the mountains behind it. They passed wagons of coal, and a fine black dust covered everything.

The coach continued through the Appalachian Mountains, and even Mrs. Post, who had traveled the road many times, stared out the window and declared it the most beautiful scenery she had ever seen. The horses labored, pulling the coach up the hills, but descending was even worse. The drivers were careful, however. They slowed the coach to a stop before starting down the steep inclines.

Luke agreed with Mrs. Post. He stared in awe at the mountains, wondering if this was what his father felt when he looked at the prairie. The mountains were so beautiful he was afraid to blink and take the chance that they were only imagination. His pencil flew over the paper, trying to capture everything he saw. He hated to stop long enough for the reading and writing lessons Uncle Eli insisted on giving him.

At every stop the conversation was about gold. "Gold fever," Uncle Eli called it. "President Polk says it's true," a bearded man proclaimed loudly to anyone listening one morning at breakfast. "A person can just walk along and pick up nuggets as big as your fist."

"It must really be true if the president says so," Luke remarked.

"Even a president can be fooled," Uncle Eli said.

On the third day they arrived in the city of Baltimore, and Uncle Eli had a surprise. "We'll finish our journey by railroad," he told Luke.

Luke could hardly hold in his excitement. Not only would he see the railroad, but he was actually going to ride on one. "I wish Caleb and Michael were here," he told Uncle Eli.

Uncle Eli gave him a comforting pat. "They'll see it in your pictures."

They spent the night at an inn. Like most they had seen along the way, this one was a large, comfortable stone house. The lower floor was the dining room. Mrs. Post ate dinner with them, and afterward the innkeeper showed them the sleeping rooms upstairs. There were several other men who were already asleep. Mrs. Post was right next door in the ladies' room.

The next morning they said good-bye to Mrs. Post. She was continuing her journey by stage. "I'll leave the trains to you young people," she said, hugging Luke good-bye. "Don't worry. I'll come to see you in Boston."

Uncle Eli hired a carriage to take them to the Mount Clare railroad station. While his uncle bought their tickets, Luke anxiously sat in the

waiting room. Every now and then he walked outside on the platform, anxious for his first glimpse
of the train. Uncle Eli bought two lunches from a
vendor at the door. "There's talk of serving meals
on the trains," he explained, "but for now we have
to bring our own food."

Uncle Eli patiently answered his questions, but
nothing could have prepared Luke for his first
sight of the engine chugging up the track toward
the station. It was a giant black monster spewing
black smoke from a huge smokestack. At the front
of the engine were an oil lantern and a large fan-
shaped iron piece. "That's called a cowcatcher,"
Uncle Eli said.

Horses hitched to wagons reared in alarm, and
the drivers fought to keep them from running
away.

"We're going to get inside of that?" Luke asked
weakly as he followed his uncle. He could see men
hastily loading a fresh supply of wood for the engine. Sparks flew in the air.

There were several passenger cars attached to
the train. Luke and Uncle Eli entered a car and
found rows of seats, most of them already full of

fellow passengers. Then with a blast from the horn they were off on the final leg of their journey.

It was exciting but frightening too. Luke gripped the edge of his seat so hard that his knuckles showed white. The train gently swayed back and forth with a clacking noise as it moved along the tracks.

Uncle Eli chuckled. Embarrassed, Luke loosened his grip and allowed himself to relax and enjoy the ride.

Luke saw two boys about Caleb's and Michael's ages teasing their sister by pulling her hair, then pretending to look the other way. A wave of homesickness swept over him. He had never before realized how big the country was, how very far away were the little sod house and his family.

Uncle Eli settled down with a newspaper, and Luke contented himself with his sketch pad. The miles flew by faster than he believed possible. In the evening they changed trains. This one had small compartments with seats that folded down to narrow sleeping ledges. Luke slept to the gently rocking clickity-clack of the wheels.

Another change of trains brought them at last

to Boston. "We made it!" Uncle Eli exclaimed. "This is your new home."

Leaving the train station, they caught a horse-drawn cab that whisked them across the city. Luke hung his head out the window and inhaled. There was a fishy smell in the air, and seagulls flew in circles over the imposing brick buildings. Uncle Eli laughed. "I missed that smell all the way across the country."

The driver took them up a hill lined with stately houses. From here Luke could look down at the harbor and the ocean. The harbor was crowded with ships. They were not like the steamboats on the river. These were huge sailing vessels with tall sails. Luke wished he could go directly to the wharf and explore.

"I need to find my partners," said Uncle Eli. "I'll take you home and you can get settled in." He directed the cab to a shady street where large houses clustered above the harbor. The cab stopped in front of a particularly ornate brick mansion.

"Is this a hotel?" Luke asked.

Uncle Eli chuckled. "This is my house."

Luke's mouth fell open. The house was bigger

than some of the hotels they had stayed in. It was on a hill, and large windows gave a view of the ocean.

A tall, elegant black woman greeted them. "Mr. Eli, you are home at last," she said, smiling. "And who is your young friend?"

"Hello, Miss Maisie. This is my nephew Luke. He is going to be staying with us at least until spring. Please put him in the blue room. And send for my tailor. Luke is going to need some new clothes.

"I will be back as soon as I can, Luke," Uncle Eli said. "Miss Maisie will take good care of you."

"It will be nice to have someone in the house again," the housekeeper said as she led Luke up a curved staircase. She pointed to a door. "That is your uncle's room. And this," she said as she opened a door across the hallway, "will be yours."

Luke took a step into the room and gasped in amazement. The room was bigger than his whole house. A huge fireplace took up one wall. Along another were a desk and shelves filled with books. There were several dressers, and in the middle of the room was the largest bed he had ever seen, covered with beautiful blue quilt. There were matching curtains on the windows. Miss Maisie pulled back the curtains and opened the windows, letting in the tangy smell of the sea.

Luke put down his bag and started to sit on the comfortable-looking bed.

"Oh, no. Not in those clothes," Miss Maisie said firmly. "First you take a bath."

Uncle Eli had a special room for a bath. The tub was white and stood on curved legs. Miss Maisie made him sit on a wooden bench while two women brought up buckets of hot water and filled the tub. Then she handed him some fresh-smelling soap and a thick, fluffy white towel. "Scrub every inch. And don't put those clothes back on. I'll find something of your uncle's for you to wear until your new clothes are ready."

Luke stepped into the tub and quickly scrubbed himself. He was reaching for the towel when Miss Maisie came back in the room. Embarrassed, he wrapped the towel around himself.

"Not so fast, young man," Miss Maisie said. "Three weeks of traveling dust don't come off in five minutes." She checked behind his ears and

sent him back with a scrub brush for his finger-
nails. At last she pronounced him clean and allowed him to dress in a pair of Uncle Eli's pants
with the legs rolled up and a shirt that reached
past his knees.

He was following Miss Maisie back to the
kitchen for a snack when Mr. Epson, the tailor,
arrived. Luke was quickly measured, and promising
to have at least one pair of trousers and a shirt
ready by morning, Mr. Epson hurried back to his
shop.

In the kitchen Miss Maisie introduced him to
Colleen, the cook, and her helper, Lettie. Colleen
was round and full of smiles, and her speech had
a soft lilt. She reminded Luke of his own mother,
and he had to fight a moment of sadness.

"It will be nice to have another hungry boy
around," Colleen said. She gave him a plate with
meat, cheese, and the softest bread he had ever
tasted. Luke was too shy to ask who the other boy
was.

While he ate, the three women asked him about
Iowa. Luke tried to describe the little sod house
and the vast prairie, wishing heartily that he could

sketch for them what was so sharply drawn in his mind. Finally he asked Colleen where she was from, and she told him about Ireland and the terrible famine that had brought her to America. "Was a blight. The potatoes rotted in the ground," she said. "People are starving. Thousands of my countrymen are coming to America. Most of them are forced to go to work in the mills or mines for so little money they might have been better off staying in Ireland." Her eyes clouded. "If not for your uncle, I would have been just like the others."

Afterward Luke wandered around his uncle's house. Outside he found a garden fragrant with roses, and a wooden chair swing under the limbs of a huge tree. He had never dreamed that Uncle Eli was so rich. He sat in the swing and closed his eyes. There had been too many new things to get used to in one day.

A rustle of leaves made him open his eyes. There in front of him was a friendly face peeping out of the bushes. Luke jumped up, too startled for words.

The face grinned, and Luke realized it was a boy not much older than he was. The brown eyes sparkled.

"Didn't mean to scare you," the boy said. He stood up, and Luke saw that he was holding a long-handled pair of hedge trimmers. Without thinking, Luke took a step backward.

The boy smiled again. "I'm Toby."

Luke had recovered from his shock. "Do you live here?"

Toby nodded. "Miss Maisie is my ma. Mr. Reed lets us live over there." He pointed to a neat carriage house in back of the main house. It was small but freshly painted, and a small vegetable garden was at the side.

"Are you a slave?" Luke blurted out.

Toby drew himself up tall. "No, sir! My ma and I are free. Mr. Reed doesn't believe in slaves. We work for him, and he pays us wages."

"I'm sorry for asking," Luke said. Relief poured over him. He did not want to think of his uncle as a slaveholder.

"I'm Luke," he said.

"I know," Toby said. "Ma already told me. I'm supposed to watch and be sure you don't get yourself in any trouble."

Now it was Luke's turn to be offended. "I don't need anyone watching over me."

Toby went back to work with the clippers. Snip, snip. Then he stopped and looked back at Luke. "Could I get myself into trouble on your farm?"

"Maybe," Luke admitted reluctantly.

"And would you show me around and warn me about things? Wild cows and things like that."

Luke smiled at the idea of wild cows, but he nodded. "All right, you win."

"So what do you want to do?" asked Toby.

Luke didn't hesitate. "I want to see the ocean. Can we go down to the docks?"

Toby frowned. "There're a lot of rough men there. I don't know if Mr. Reed would like us going by ourselves."

"Then let's go now before he gets back and says no," Luke said. He told Toby about the new letter of sketches he was making for his family.

"You want to go to the ocean and draw it?" Toby exclaimed, sounding incredulous. Then he shrugged. "We'll have to hurry. And don't tell Ma where we are going. She'll have a conniption for sure."

Luke ran upstairs and got his tablet and crayons. Toby showed him out a small gate at the back of the yard. He led the way through twisted alleys and cobblestoned streets toward the wharf. While they walked, Luke told Toby about the farm and his family.

"See that hill right there?" Toby asked.

Luke spun around. "What hill?"

Toby grinned. "There used to be a hill there. Every time they run out of room here, they chop down a hill and dump it along the shore. They just keep making Boston bigger and bigger."

They had reached the docks, and Luke stood still, gasping in amazement.

"It's wonderful!" he exclaimed. Far out in the bay tall-masted ships unfurled their sails, ready for their next voyage. There were shops along some of the docks. Other docks were piled with goods ready for shipment—whale oil for lamps, machinery, furniture, and cloth from the nearby mills. Burly sailors speaking strange languages unloaded other ships from afar. At one end of the bay was a busy shipyard. Luke could see workers scurrying over the towering skeleton of a ship taking shape to join her sisters at sea. In another place teenage boys cleaned and salted codfish. It was smelly, hard work, but Toby told him they made only twenty-five cents a day.

"Mr. Reed pays me fifty cents a day," Toby said proudly.

Luke had never even had one half dollar to call his own. "Is everyone in Boston rich?" he asked.

"Not me," Toby said ruefully. "Ma makes me save it all. She says I'm going to college. Mr. Reed helps me with my Latin when he's home. Maybe we can study together."

Luke felt his face go red. "I guess I'll have to get better at reading American first."

"Don't worry," Toby said, seeing his embarrassment. "Mr. Reed will have you reading in no time at all. He's a mighty fine teacher. If he hadn't been so rich, I believe he'd've been a schoolmaster."

Luke shook his head. He was certainly learning a lot about his uncle that he had never known.

The boys stood at the end of a dock, looking out at the ocean. Luke had decided the mountains were the prettiest thing he'd seen, but now he wasn't so sure. White-capped waves gently rocked against the docks. And everywhere were the gulls, scolding as they darted among the sailors.

There was a large log on the sand, bleached nearly white from the ocean. Without a word Luke headed straight for it, sat, and began to sketch.

FOURTEEN

---·---

Kidnapped!

For a time Toby amused himself watching over Luke's shoulder as he drew. After a while he grew bored and wandered closer to the docks. He read posters pinned outside some of the shops and came back to tell Luke what they said. "There's a bunch of posters advertising trips to California," he reported. "Fast ships and experienced crews. Travel in comfort and luxury. Only three hundred dollars for a chance to become a rich man," Toby recited.

Luke nodded absently. "Most people are going by wagon. We saw lots of them on our trip."

Toby sighed. "Not much chance that I'll ever see any of that gold."

Luke did not answer, and Toby wandered back to the docks and contented himself with looking at the goods stacked on pallets ready for shipment to all parts of the country. There were coffee and sugar from the West Indies and silks and porcelain from China. From time to time he returned to watch Luke.

"Almost done," Luke said each time.

"This is great," Toby said. "I don't know why Ma always worries about my coming here."

Luke nodded, but it was obvious he was not really listening.

"We have to get back soon," Toby reminded him. "Ma will tan my hide if I don't get you back for supper."

Luke finally looked up. "Just a few more minutes," he begged.

Toby shrugged and wandered off again. Luke looked up from his drawing and noticed Toby suddenly wheel around and stare at a sailor sitting on the deck of a nearby sloop.

Toby walked back to Luke. "I had this creepy

feeling like someone was watching me," he reported.

Luke looked around. The sailor had disappeared. It was late enough that many of the dockworkers were quitting for the day, saying good-bye to their friends and trudging wearily away from the busy port.

Toby sat quietly for a time, but he was a boy who did not like sitting still. Now he walked along the water's edge, where he contented himself throwing pebbles out to sea.

"Like ships, do you?" a voice said. It was the sailor Toby had noticed before. He was smiling in a friendly way.

"Yes, sir," Toby answered politely. "But mostly I'm waiting for my friend."

The man raised one eyebrow. "Friend? Not master?"

"I am a free person," Toby said.

"Well, that is fine," the man said.

Far down at the edge of the docks Luke looked up from his drawing at them and then went back to his work. "What's your friend doing?" the sailor asked.

"He's drawing the ocean," Toby answered. "This is the first time he has seen it."

"Well, he seems to have forgotten you. I've noticed how he makes you wait for him. Would you like to come on my ship and take a look? Captain's gone ashore to one of the grogshops. I can show you around quick before he comes back."

"I think my friend is almost done," Toby said reluctantly. He was curious to see inside one of the ships.

"It's not far," the sailor said. "You'll be back before he notices you're gone."

That seemed true enough. Luke was bent over his paper, frowning in concentration.

Luke was nearly finished with the drawing. He added a gull on a corner of the page with its curved bill tearing at a bit of bread. Then he stood up and stretched.

"Done," he said, looking at the picture with satisfaction. Every inch of the paper was filled with the sights along the harbor.

He looked up. Where was Toby? The last time

he'd seen him he had been talking to a pretty rough-looking sailor.

Luke waited patiently, feeling a little guilty. The sun was getting low in the sky, and he realized he'd been drawing for hours. This was no way to treat a new friend. He would make it up to him, Luke vowed to himself. Tomorrow they would do whatever Toby wanted to do, and this time he would leave his tablet at home.

The sun had dipped lower and lower on the horizon. Miss Maisie was going to be upset. Where was Toby anyway? It seemed as if a long time had passed since Luke had seen him. He wandered along the dock, clutching his drawing.

Suppose Toby had given up and gone home? But that was unlikely. Especially when Uncle Eli had asked him to watch over his nephew. Maybe Toby was angry because he'd ignored him all afternoon, and this was his way of getting even. Maybe he was close by, secretly laughing at Luke's worry. Luke discarded that theory too. Toby had not seemed that upset, and anyway, he would not continue the joke when it was so late.

Luke's concern grew by the minute. He stopped

several passersby and described Toby. People shook their heads and hurried away, busy with their own problems.

It was almost dark when he finally admitted to himself that something was seriously wrong.

He sat back down on the log and tried to think. How could he find his uncle and ask him for help? He knew he would never find the house again through all those twisted streets.

He suddenly remembered seeing a watchman at various times through the afternoon patrolling the wharves. He ran up and down the water's edge looking down each of the long docks. At last he spotted the watchman near a fish market on the longest wharf.

The man gave him a curious look as Luke ran toward him. "What is the trouble, lad? You look pale enough to have seen a ghost."

"My friend has disappeared. I think something might have happened to him."

Words went tumbling one over another as he blurted out his story.

"I'm sure your friend is fine. He's probably home right now, laughing at his big joke."

"He wouldn't do that. I know something has happened to him," Luke said.

"Maybe your friend ran off to sea," said the watchman. "Boys do that, you know. Maybe your friend was looking for a little adventure." The watchman put his arm around Luke's shoulder in a friendly manner. "You'd better be getting home. It's not safe here at night."

"I just moved in with my uncle," Luke said. "Without Toby I won't be able to find my way back to his house."

"And who might your uncle be?"

"Eli Reed," Luke said.

"Eli Reed is your uncle? He's a fine gentleman."

"You know him?" Luke asked. "Can you give me directions to his house?"

The watchman suddenly chuckled. "I'll do better than that. I'll take you to him."

"Oh, thank—," Luke started to say. Then, as he turned, he caught sight of his uncle striding down the dock. He did not look happy.

Uncle Eli," Luke cried. He ran to him and threw his arms around his waist.

Luke quickly told his story. "The watchman doesn't believe that Toby is missing. He thinks he just ran away to sea."

The watchman looked embarrassed. "I didn't know the boy worked for you, Mr. Reed. I'd be glad to search for him. It's growing late, though, and as you can see, he could be anywhere."

"My nephew says he was talking to a sailor," Uncle Eli said.

"There are a hundred ships here. And a thousand sailors," the watchman said sourly. He flashed a quick look at Luke and said quietly, "Sometimes boys are kidnapped and forced to serve on ships."

"Then we'd better find him fast," Uncle Eli said grimly.

The watchman sighed. "What about the sailor? Did you get a good look at him, lad?"

"He had long brown hair tied in the back and he was thin, and rough-looking," Luke answered. "Wait! I drew him."

Luke unrolled his picture and pointed to one of the sketches. The watchman studied it. "That could be Little Jake," he said thoughtfully. "Wouldn't put something like this past him. Meaner than a snake." The watchman suddenly snapped his fingers. "Jake was looking for a cabin boy today."

"You know him, then?" Uncle Eli asked.

"First mate on the *Savannah*. It's a little ship that does business in the South. Just brought a load of cotton for the mills at Lowell. Jake's been telling anyone who'd listen that they were sailing for California this time, like everyone else. Said they wouldn't be back for a year. He was bragging about how rich he was going to be."

"Let's go find this Little Jake," said Uncle Eli.

The watchman still looked glum. "I don't know where the *Savannah* was berthed. It will take forever to search all the docks."

"No," Luke said thoughtfully. "When I sketched him, I was sitting near the end of the harbor." Luke pointed where he meant. "He and some other men were on a dock unloading cotton. The ship can't be far."

Praying he was right, Luke led them to the dock where he'd seen the men.

"There she is," said Uncle Eli, pointing to the very last ship.

"They're getting ready to sail," grunted the watchman, hurrying to keep up with Uncle Eli's long-legged stride. "We're too late."

It was true. The loading ramp had been pulled in, and Luke could see several sailors turning the winch to pull up the anchor.

"Ahoy, the *Savannah*," the watchman called loudly.

One of the sailors on the winch came to the side.

"Let me speak to your captain," the watchman shouted.

The sailor nodded and disappeared. A minute later he was back with a sloppy-looking round-bellied man. His captain's coat was unbuttoned, and his speech was slurred.

"What do you want?" he growled.

"We have reason to believe that a boy in my employment is on your ship," Uncle Eli shouted.

"A runaway, eh? We know how to deal with those." The captain chuckled.

Luke shivered, wondering at the fate of any runaways who would be found by such an awful man.

"Not a runaway. We think he may have been

kidnapped by your first mate Little Jake," the watchman called.

The captain's eyes narrowed, and his eyes looked crafty. "I'm sure you"re mistaken. Jake Morgan is an honest sailor. He wouldn't kidnap anyone."

"Then you wouldn't mind our coming on board and making a search?" called the watchman.

"I would," the Captain answered. "We're already late setting out."

Uncle Eli's eyes grew steely. "I am a powerful man," he said. "One word from me and no one will ever buy your goods. I suggest you let us on board."

The captain seemed to consider. Luke whispered to Uncle Eli, "Is that true? Are you that powerful?"

Uncle Eli winked. "Probably not. But as long as he believes it, we might have a chance."

The captain was talking to another man who'd come up on deck. "That's him," Luke said. "That's the man Toby was talking to this afternoon."

The captain was arguing with his first mate, but his back was turned, and they couldn't hear what was said. A minute later the first mate disappeared and the captain looked over the rail. "It was all a misunderstanding," he shouted. "Jake thought the boy was a runaway. He was trying to be kind and offer him gainful employment."

"There's no way to prove otherwise," the watchman muttered. "But I'm sure he knew the boy was not a runaway."

"There he is," Luke shouted. Toby had appeared at the side. His hands were bound, and he walked with a shuffle, as though his feet were also tied.

"Send the boy to shore, and that will be the end of it," Uncle Eli called.

There was more conversation on board. The ship was aready too far away from the dock to put out the ramp, but after several anxious moments a small boat was lowered and a sailor rowed a battered and bruised but otherwise whole Toby to shore.

"We'll be watching you when you come to port again," the watchman shouted.

"It was an honest mistake." The captain shoved Jake, knocking him to the deck. "You can be sure that I'll punish my first mate."

"Punish him for getting caught, you mean," Uncle Eli muttered under his breath.

Toby stumbled onshore, and Uncle Eli hugged him. "Are you all right?" he asked.

"Yes, sir," Toby said. "But I am mighty grateful to you for rescuing me."

"You can thank Luke here. It was his pictures that saved you," Uncle Eli said.

"It was my pictures that got him in trouble in the first place," Luke said.

"We'll talk about that when we get home," Uncle Eli said. And to Toby he added, "I can imagine your mother is going to have a few things to say to you too."

The boys hung their heads. "Yes, sir," they said together.

Uncle Eli hesitated. "You see that ship over there?" He pointed to a small clipper ship. The hull was unpainted, and the sails were dirty and torn. But beneath all that was a trim, graceful shape that spoke of what she must have looked like in the past.

"She's ours," said Uncle Eli. "I bought her this afternoon. We're going to use her to take a load of useful things to California. The shipyard is going to rent me some space to refurbish her. We'll make her as good as new."

"You mean you're leaving again?" Luke said. "What will I do?"

"You'll go to school," Uncle Eli said sternly. Then a twinkle came in his eye, and he winked. "I imagine there would be a lot of new things to draw on an ocean voyage. I suppose I could hire a schoolteacher for the trip. There's probably one or two who wouldn't mind searching for gold."

Luke looked at his uncle. He was hardly able to believe his ears. "You mean I could go too?"

"It will take a couple of months to get her ready, but I see I can't leave you at home and expect you to stay out of mischief. Toby either, for that matter."

Toby's eyes lit up, and he grinned at Luke.

"Of course, that's up to Miss Maisie, but I'll point out to her that a schoolteacher might as well have two students." Uncle Eli put one arm around each boy as they headed back home. "Maybe Miss Maisie would like to come too," he added thoughtfully. He looked at Toby. "I suspect your mother is not going to be happy with you two tonight. My advice is to wait a few days before you mention an ocean voyage."

Uncle Eli hailed a cab pulled by four sleek black horses, and a few minutes later they were moving swiftly up the hill toward home.

"I heard a new song today," Uncle Eli said. To the cabdriver's amazement he bellowed it out, only slightly off-key.

> "Oh! Susanna, don't you cry for me;
> I'm bound for California
> With my banjo on my knee."

Covering their ears, Toby and Luke grinned at each other, thinking of the adventures ahead. There was one thing both of them understood: Any adventure was better when shared with a friend.

More about *Luke*

Eighteen-forty-nine signaled a great change for America. People from every walk of life left their jobs and homes and struck out for California to make their fortunes. Soldiers deserted their posts, sailors abandoned ships in the harbor, shopkeepers left their stores, and farmers their fields, all for a chance at finding gold. The news soon spread to other countries, whose people joined the madness. Even those few skeptics were convinced when President James Polk (1795–1849), believing an exaggerated report, announced that the stories were true. Thousands made the trip overland, braving disease and Indian attacks, crossing deserts and mountains to reach the goldfields.

Here are some interesting facts about Luke's time:

Mr. Reed believed there would always be buffalo on the prairie, and no wonder. Huge herds—estimated from twelve to thirty million—provided food, shelter, and even clothing for the Plains Indians. The white settlers slaughtered them by the thousands for "sport," often shooting them from passing trains. A few short years later there were only twenty-three buffalo left. Fortunately they were rescued from extinction, and now several small herds roam the West under government protection.

Peddlers like Rufus Tansy played an important part in the lives of pioneers like the Reed family. Not only did they bring goods to sell, but they were also often the only source of the latest news and gossip. Many peddlers also sharpened knives and made shoes. Did you know that shoes in those days had no right or left? Both were made exactly the same and could be switched back and forth to make them wear longer.

Do you remember how nice it was when you got your first box of crayons, with their beautiful colors and pointed tips? Children in Luke's time made their own drawing materials. Charcoal from wood fires was messy but good for drawing, and colors could be made from berries or by boiling the bark from certain trees. Although pastels (sticks of powdered pigments bound with gum) and crayons (pigments bound with wax) were invented before 1849, they would have been a rare treat for a child out on the prairie.

Luke and his brothers liked to play baseball. The game was introduced to America about 1834 and quickly became popular. The rules were the same then, except that the bases were run in a clockwise direction and you could put a runner out by throwing the ball and hitting him. Luckily balls then were not as hard as they are today, although they were made pretty much the same way. Children wrapped string into a big ball and then talked their mothers into sewing a leather cover for it. Gloves were not used until 1875.

Cholera is caused by unsanitary conditions, especially polluted water. At the same time as the Gold Rush there were several bad outbreaks of this deadly disease. Many pioneers crossing the country in wagon trains died, some after being ill less than a day. Even President Polk died of cholera just three months after leaving office.

Most stagecoaches were called Concords. Nine people could ride inside on three padded benches. The coaches were often quite beautiful, brightly colored with scrollwork or landscapes painted on the doors. At crossroads the stagecoach drivers followed signposts made in the shape of pointing fingers to tell the direction.

In the early days of the country, if you received a letter, you would have to pay the postage. In 1847 the post office started making stamps for the sender to purchase. The first stamps looked much like those today. There was a five-cent stamp with Benjamin Franklin's picture. This was for mail going less than five hundred miles. For mail going over five hundred miles there was a ten-cent stamp with George Washington's picture. The stamps had glue backings, but the clerk had to cut them apart with scissors.

In West Virginia Luke and Uncle Eli passed the Wheeling bridge. It was completed shortly after their trip—in December 1849. Held up by wire cables, the beautiful structure was the longest suspension bridge in the world. The builders, however, did not do a very good job. A few years after completion a windstorm started waves of motion in the cables. The waves grew and grew until the bridge itself heaved and buckled and twisted so hard it fell into the river. It was rebuilt, correctly this time, but by then even longer suspension bridges had been built.